Letters From Spirit
A Bridge Between The Worlds
Marian Young Starnes

Terra Nova

Rev. Marian Y. Starnes
Terra Nova Center
3475 Reasonover Road
Cedar Mountain, NC 28718

8

ISBN 0-9654760-0-6
Printed In The United States

Cover design by Patricia Lynn Young
Book Design and Production by Terra Nova Publishing

CONTENTS

Part I
Letters From Summerland - The James Saga

Part II
Reflections On The Art of Living and Dying

Read not to criticize nor confute,
nor to believe or take for granted.
But to weigh and consider.

Benton

Dedication

*This book is humbly dedicated to the
memory of
James Richard Sollenberger.
His selfless, unconditional love not
only enriched the lives of all who were
fortunate enough to know him, but,
also left behind a powerful legacy of
hope. He was the quiet exemplar to
the end as he showed us all how to
face death with dignity and the expectation
of a glorious new life "beyond the veil".
In his living and his dying
he proved
"love never dies; it is forever".*

FORWARD

Marian Starnes has been my personal and spiritual friend for many years. I know her to be both warrior and sage in her tireless quest for Divine Truth. Beyond which, she lives the corporal works of mercy. In the best Christ-like tradition, Marian feeds the hungry, clothes the naked, gives drink to the thirsty, visits the sick and buries the dead. Now, she's gone a step beyond, to provide comforting insight into the life of the soul after death itself.

Over the years, I've watched Marian follow her convictions about the goodness of God with near perfect faith. One of my favorite conversations with her comes to mind: Shortly after she'd followed her guidance to found the spiritual retreat center, Terra Nova, only to be beset by enough financial woes and unexpected problems to unnerve Job, Marian told me how she'd coped with such adversity. " I went out into the yard, Cathy", she said with robust conviction. "I shook my fist at Heaven and I said I don't care what you do to me, God, you'll never shake my faith in your goodness!" It seemed to me the ultimate act of love and belief. You can't rail at God if you don't believe in Him, *bigtime.*

Marian lives what she teaches. Love God, love your fellow man, be the best human being you can be, and trust that the Divine Father/Mother will see you through. Pray, Love, Forgive, Teach, Hold the Grand Vision, this is how she describes her mission, and she fulfills it to the letter.

Marian also has the distinction of being one of the only two mystics I know (and I know quite a few heavy-hitters), who has never yet been wrong in what she's culled from the psychic airwaves for me.

If you can't know Marian as I am privileged to, the next best thing I can wish for you is that you read her book. Not only will her conversations with her beloved James give you fascinating insight into what happens to the soul after physical death, but the Q & A section will answer many of those niggling questions you were probably longing for a lifetime to ask someone with a direct line to Heaven.

Her knowledge will astound you. Her compassion and love will enfold you. Do your self a favor. Let her be your *Bridge between the Worlds*, you'll find yourself bathed in the loveliest Light.

Cathy Cash-Spellman
Author of
Paint The Wind
Bless the Child
The Playground of the Gods

No Grave Will Ever Contain You

"Marian"

Startled, I looked up from the casket being lowered into the dark grave. Torn from the depths of my mourning, I looked around. Everyone that was gathered on this sad day was contained within their own grief. My beloved grandmother was being buried there under the tall pines in a little north Idaho cemetery. Save for the drone of the ministers voice and the silent weeping of friends and family, all was quiet.

"Marian, over here"

The voice, so familiar, so dear, spoke a little louder now. Without turning, I glanced around, wondering if the rest of them had heard the voice. But no, no one seemed to hear.

"Marian, look at me!"

The voice was urgent now. I looked to my right, and in shock I could only stare! It was her, Grandma, standing in front of the small cemetery shed, wearing her best blue dress, smiling at me!

But, it can't be. Grandma's body dressed in that same blue dress, had moments earlier been lowered into the grave. The apparition spoke my name again. Stunned, I looked away from her to the casket, and she said " I am not there. Just as no grave will ever contain you, I am not there. Remember this, and remember I have always loved you and will always be near you. Only the body dies, but it is nothing. I know you do not understand, but some day you will and you will teach this to thousands of people".

My mouth fell open and I wanted to scream, can't you see her? Can't you hear her? But the sigh of the wind and quiet sobs were the only sounds that day. They had heard nothing.

Reality shattered, I looked around again, and she was gone. Was this my imagination? Had I imagined such a thing, while lost inside my grief?

The year was 1939. I was thirteen years old and I could tell no one. I knew what they would say, they would say that I was crazy, crazy like Grandma. I wasn't sure exactly, but I had heard the whispers and doublespeak about Grandma. I suspected it had to do with the way she talked freely about the many strange things that share this mysterious world with us, the spirits, fairies and the little ones. I began to wonder if maybe I was crazy too? Did I really see her? Had she really spoken to me?

Over the years the memory faded and passed into a forgotten corner of my mind. A few times in lectures concerning death and the lives hereafter I would spontaneously share small bits and pieces of this truth I had learned so long ago. The truth I have come to so fully understand...

"No Grave Will Ever Contain You"

The Wake Up Call

Many years later, on October 4, 1973, a near-death experience brought back the long ago words of my Grandmother, and let me visit for a brief moment the Heavenly Realms. In an operating room in Charlotte, N.C., I *"died"* for four minutes when my heart stopped, and in that moment my life changed forever.

I found myself floating above the operating table, listening to the frantic voices of the doctors and nurses. I could not relate in any way to the hectic drama or the empty body below.

I did not recognize the body lying there as being in any way *me*. How could it be? I was up *here...* just an observer. If I had any emotion at all, it was disinterest in the whole frantic scene below me. The very moment disinterest arose, I felt myself moving at an incredible speed through the ceiling, up, up, up into a wondrous Light that was urging me forward. I felt free, happy and excited! My body... for I *did* have a body.. was pain free, light, and full of vibrant life. So very different than when I entered the hospital a few days before. Gone was the heaviness, fear and excruciating pains I had been experiencing. I was free!

In a split second I was walking in the most beautiful green meadow I had ever seen. The sun shone brightly, warm, but not too hot, the birds were singing and a soft breeze touched my cheek. To my right, a giant oak tree spread it's huge branches invitingly, and for a moment I was tempted to go sit in its shade.

I heard voices off to my left, like a group of happy people just enjoying themselves. Turning, I saw a sparkling blue stream flowing toward the forest beyond the meadow. On the far side of the water, I saw a group of people waiting, laughing and I knew somehow they were waiting for *me*. There stood my father, gone from the earth so many years, looking young and so very alive, and alongside him was a small boy. Immediately, I knew that boy was my childhood friend, Harold, who was killed when we were both six years old... over forty years ago! So many friends, family and my beloved grandmother, smiling, and waiting! I started toward the foot bridge, moving without effort as radiantly happy as a child on Christmas morning! As I started across the bridge two men barred my way. They both looked Christ-like, and they smiled, calling me by name, enfolding me in their love!

The Being on the left turned to talk to the One on the right, and I knew I was the subject of discussion. He said I had suffered much and had earned the right to be there; the second Being agreed, but seemed to have *some* reservations about it. The one that spoke for me finally said, "Well, ask her." Turning toward me, the other one looked so deeply into my eyes he seemed to scan my soul, then said:

*"Beloved one, you have earned the right to come home, and if you choose, we will all welcome you and rejoice. However, long have you prepared to serve the Creator through service to your fellow man. You have the gift of teaching in a simple, loving way. So many hunger in your world for Truth and Love. You can be of great help to them: I must tell you that if you choose to return there will be great help from the angels, **but suffering, grief and pain will still be experienced** as you continue your earthly journey. You can be of tremendous service there. Will you go back, knowing the full truth of what you face? Will you love and feed our children"?*

His compassion and tenderness was overwhelming. So peaceful. His eyes, all knowing and loving, searched my soul. How could I refuse Him?

"I will go back"!

Instantly, I was back in that empty body, later awakening in a recovery room, fully aware of my experience. Even today, so many years later, the memory is etched into my being as if it only happened a few moments ago. I tried to tell people, but they thought I was rambling out of my head. Appeasing me, they just nodded in silent agreement. But I knew they didn't believe me.

Leaving the hospital ten days later, I continued to ponder the experience. I knew it was real! It was there and then, I remembered the words spoken so long ago by my Grandmother,

"No grave will ever contain you"!

I remembered!

I believed!

And my search was on!

Where Have They Gone?

A loved one dies. Grief, hopelessness, and depression hang like a heavy pall over the ones left behind. Friends and family search for words to comfort, but so often the consoling words seem weak and empty. So many questions.

"Where have they gone?"

"How can someone be alive and then just stop being?"

"Is there really a heaven world, do Angels truly exist there?"

"Does my loved one still love me?"

"Where have they gone?"

"Will I ever meet them again?"

"Are they still a part of my life? Are they even aware of what is happening to those of us left behind?"

"What are they doing now?"

"O, God, where are they?"

Each of us have asked these questions when a loved one has left us through the death experience.

I wrote this book because the communications from James seemed to answer so much of the mystery of the After life. I found him still very much aware of our day to day problems, and that he still felt he was a vital part of our family.

His new world sounded "normal" and just like this one, but without the anger, fear and pain. His new understandings gave birth to a great surge of hope and joy! Perhaps, beyond this present existence there really is a beautiful *"Paradise"* just waiting for our Homecoming!

This book is not written to convince you of *anything*. It is written in the hope that it may answer a few of the questions that surround this process of life called death. Maybe it will inspire you to search until you find the fear of dying falling away, and the birthing of a far greater awareness than ever before.

If in any way it brings you comfort, then it has all been worthwhile.

Marian Young Starnes

Acknowledgments

There are far too many people to individually name them all on this short page. There were hundreds of people, family and friends who kept urging me to write this story even when everything in me wanted to just let it go. *You know who you are.* Every word of your encouragement and loving interest contributed to this book. To you, unsung and un-named, I thank you from the bottom of my heart.

My gratitude to Patricia Lynn Young who spent tireless hours putting this book together; to Karla Powell and Brenda Peoples who did the original transcriptions from my jumbled notes. And a special thank-you to: Lianne B. Starnes who never stopped believing I could do it; to Mary Lemons Pridmore whose constant encouragement kept me going; Cathy Cash Spellman, Josseph and Alice Rynear, Tu Moonwalker, Lané Sáan, Janice O'Neill, Virginia and Jerry Shuford, Carolyn B. Christie, Kathryn Ann Thomas, Rachel Blalock, Robert H. Gunter, Joe D. Mayes, James and Salle Redfield, Dr. Peter Campbell, Beverly Planck, Vivien Minier and all the others who held out helping hands during the painful, stress filled time of bringing this book to life.

And a special recognition to my family who "kept me going" in the darkest hours of my grief. Without their encouragement the fear of "going public" with these letters would have been overwhelming. I express gratitude to my daughter Carole, who did not give me empty platitudes, but just was there; to my son, Troy, who's quiet strength sustained us all during the writing of this manuscript. To Phillip and Alisha who brought joy and laughter into our lives, and didn't think their grandmother was crazy.

And lastly, to David Bruce Starnes who, also, managed to "cross the barriers" between Here and There. Though the singer died, his song still lives on in the hearts of all of us.

Introduction

James and I were only married a brief *three and a half months*. My world turned upside down when he suddenly died. Still in the "honeymoon stage" of our relationship I was totally unprepared to face life without him. Tremendous shock, doubts and denial mixed with confusion and over whelming grief literally crippled me emotionally. Over and over I silently screamed "why, why"?

For the first few weeks, I was scarcely aware of anything around me. Wrung out emotionally, mentally confused and spiritually over-whelmed with questions and doubts, I struggled to try to make sense out of what had happened. This just wasn't the way we had planned it!

Both James and I had a strong faith, believing that as spiritual be-ings we could never *really* die. We knew the bodies died, but we both believed the "tenant" never did. We talked much during his illness about what lay beyond the veil, and the possibility of communication between the two worlds. We felt our love was so strong that death could not destroy it. And we were positive that we would never again lose one another even if one of us did have to leave first.

It was a second marriage for both of us. After spending many years alone we entered into the great miracle of our love radiantly happy. We constantly were amazed at how much we thought and felt alike; it was un-canny how we each knew each others thoughts and feelings! We talked about "other lifetimes" that we felt we'd shared together. We simply "knew" one another far beyond the experiences of this lifetime. It is said that the soul never forgets those it has loved before; I now *know* that this is the truth.

As personalities, we were a perfect study in contrasts. He was a tall man, well over six foot, soft spoken, mannerly and deeply introspective. I stand five three and a half, am down to earth, "across the kitchen table friendly", outgoing and spontaneous. He was the thoughtful *observer* of

Life, while I managed to be right in the middle of the *action*.

We both loved books. He read philosophy and the classics. I read everything I could get my hands on, and for special fun, Louis L'Amour. He adored symphonic music, operas, and classical recordings. While I loved all music, I especially liked Patsy Cline, The Statler Brothers, and Jim Reeves. He disliked going to the movies, I found them delightful diversions. He wasn't comfortable unless the room was eighty degrees or more, I was miserable if it got over seventy. (He often teased me by calling my room the arctic).

But, as the unique patterning of left and right hands, we fit together like a pair of comfortable old gloves. He was an Aquarian and I a Cancer, and in spite of the books that said we couldn't, we found a grand compatibility together. We first met when I was teaching in New Mexico in the 80's, and immediately became fast friends. We shared our spiritual journey and our love for God and slowly he began to "catch" some of my zest for life! Finally, friendship grew into a wonderful love. He left New Mexico and moved to Charlotte, N.C., where I was living. It wasn't long before we were married, pledging to love each other "forever and ever".

When the following messages started coming, I was still frozen in grief, and definitely in no space to be open to anything, *seen or unseen*, that would further shake up my fragile emotions. My initial reaction was anger, rejection and outright denial. And then through a series of "signs", like a book flying off the table for no reason at all, the CD player coming on by itself, and then feeling an actual touch on my shoulder when no one was present, I finally agreed to "listen". Six weeks after his death the signs (or signals) began. I became increasingly aware of his presence, once even smelling his favorite Lagerfelt cologne. The awarenesses were always followed by the sound of his voice in my head, saying "write", "please, please, write". Then he appeared in a dream and asked me to "please let him in" because he had an important message for humanity.

Once the messages started, I would "see" James's eyes looking at me intensely as I wrote. At first I felt foolish, and I was afraid people would think the grief had "pushed me over the edge". What if they all thought I was crazy? *And, at that point, I wasn't so very sure that I wasn't!* But, after about a dozen "transmissions" a sense of peace and joy began to enfold me as I wrote, transporting me beyond the pain. As doubts faded, I began to "know", and finally became convinced of the validity of his messages.

James reported that he was in a beautiful place which is known as the Third Heaven. That is the spiritual plane, or heaven from which the soul no longer has need to re-enter this great university of life called planet earth. No further embodiments in our physical world of form and matter are necessary. The soul now learns and serves on a higher plane.

The first messages were intensely personal in his efforts to comfort and guide me with family relationships and day-to-day living. For that reason I have omitted them, since they were of no concern to anyone except myself. Therefore, I have started with the first of the letters that contain any information that might interest those who long to know what lies beyond the veil.

In the times of my deepest dispair I angrily tore into tiny shreds many of his messages, and was not able to retrieve them later. I regret that I did this, but these are the letters I did manage to hang on to. To the best of my ability I have presented them exactly as they were received. Most of the letters were received in a six month period in 1991 and 1992. Then only an occasional message would come through, often from Radha*, rather than from James. A two year period sped by quickly. During this time there were no further attempts, on my part, to communicate with James, as I was recovering from all of the grief and pain I had experienced. However in late 1994 James again began to communicate from time to time regarding the enormous changes in consciousness that are now being faced here on earth.

I would like to add that the initial communications were emotional, and often erratic. Only after I became comfortable in the writing did really valuable "other world" information begin to come through. As we progressed, a bigger picture of Summerland started to unfold. I would think of so many things I'd plan to ask him, but once the transmission started I literally would "freeze" and seem "brain-dead" and none of the important queries would be forthcoming.

So it is with great love and humility that I share Letters from Summerland with you, dear reader.

---

* The Master Teacher responsible for helping to "open the door" so that these messages were possible.

What is this thing called death?

From childhood on, I've pondered this question, and as the years have passed my concepts have changed many times, as I've continued to grow spiritually. After the experience in the cemetery with my grandmother, for many years I wavered between fear and dread of the Unknown, and an insatiable desire to see what lay beyond the veil. I read many books on the subject, finding gems of truth and insight, but none satisfying the yearning to really "know". I *knew* that there was so much more, just waiting to be discovered. The keys to understanding couldn't be in some far off hidden place, maybe they were right here in the heart of every human being... including me!

In October 1969 I "met" my first true spiritual teacher on the side of a mountain in North Carolina. While in a deep meditative state, a kindly, white haired gentleman dressed in simple white robes approached me. He said his name was The Ancient One called Love. He stated that he had come to answer my questions, teach me, and give me the opportunity to pass those wisdoms on to others! To say that I was startled would be an understatement! Frightened yet at the same time drawn to his quiet peaceful love, I agreed to at least listen. He appeared to me to be so real; it was a long time before I realized that I was seeing him not in this third dimensional reality, but on another plane altogether. Over the next seven years we "met" many times. The truths he shared were loving, simple and practical. I found myself gently being led away from my former God-fearing attitudes and self-rightiousness into a new God-loving consiousness.

Early on he placed his hands, one on top of my head, and the other on my forehead. I felt each time he did this that I was being greatly blessed, as shock waves of pure energy filled my whole body! When I asked him what was happening to me, he said it was necessary for him to activate long forgotten knowledge and to empower me to do the task at hand.

What task? To teach others to overcome their fears about God, and especially about death! How? He said he would teach me. Why me? He said "Why not." He said that I would now be able to share ideas, thoughts, and philosophies verbally, whenever I was asked! And later I would write of these things.

When I heard his words it truly frightened me, for I had always been a shy, lonely person who found solace in books. The thought of speaking before strangers was terrifying, indeed! His answer to this was to place his hands on my heart and my throat, flooding me with powerful charges of energy. I felt like I was caught in an electrical current! God, was he trying to kill me? Reading my troubled thoughts, he smiled into my eyes, and quietly said "No, dear one, I am removing your blockages of fear, so that you can freely speak!"

He asked that I seek no publicity or advertising, but let Spirit lead those to me that I might be able to help. His suggestion, for he never ordered, was to set aside a time each week for prayer and the study of philosophy and spiritual concepts. In prayer, I would, thereby, open a "channel" to Higher Consciousness, and the words of hope, peace, love, clarity, and understanding would flow from me, as he put it, "like a river".

There were three of us, all friends, who started to meet at my home on Wednesday nights and do as he asked. By word of mouth, people, mostly young people, heard about our meetings and they asked to come. The more questions they asked, the more that powerful words of Truth and Love came through me! And so it is, even to this day. As I shared, I too was being taught.

The biggest question, and most frequently asked, was about the cycles of life and death. The answers always came around to the same thing...*there is no death*! We are spirit, that never dies, but only changes. We are spiritual entities who happen to have a body: not bodies that have a spirit stashed somewhere! Life is like a big school for gods, and lifetime after lifetime the spirit chooses many different experiences in order to learn to become the gods that we are meant to be. Death is only a doorway to release us from bondage so we can return Home for more learning! On and on, over the years, The Ancient One continued to "stretch" my awareness of our own immortality!

By the time the "James saga" began to unfold, I had long ago learned to quiet my outer mind, and listen to the soft, clear voice within. Guided often by visions, and spiritual journeys out of my body, I knew he had taught me a tremendous truth. The more I overcame my own fears of dying, the more I found myself comforting and counseling the bereaved and terminally ill. And, underlying it all, was the intense desire to penetrate the veil of sorrow, dread and fear that death instills in all of us.

What is this thing called Death? I believe it is the most loving gift possible from God! *A ticket Home*, to peace, harmony and joy, after our experiences in the duality of physical embodiment, with all it's pains and strifes. After James's wonderful description, I knew that death really was an act of great Grace from a compassionate and all loving Creator! I came to know we never die, we only evolve!

NOTE: What did I feel as I received these transmissions from James, and later, from his teacher, Radha? In the beginning I felt *resentment* at the intrusion into my grief! But, slowly I began to realize something very special was happening. Each time the strong urge to pick up the pen came, I felt a great peace and joy, although after the session, the numbness of grief's dispair usually returned. I would re-read the messages, confused, wanting to believe, but so personally involved in the process it was difficult to know what was happening.

During this time, The Ancient One came in a dream, and assured me I had not lost my mind! He reminded me of the message from my grandmother so many years before, and of the encounter with the Christ in 1973. He said now was the time to, as he put it, *complete the mission*! He told me the messages were not just for my own healing, but to encourage and help many, many people through the dark abyss of grief and dispair.

Amazingly at no time did I ever want to die and go "join James", though I felt every possible emotion from shock, grief, resentment, disbelief, and denial. At last, peace slowly began to flood my being; I knew in my heart of hearts, God, in the guise of my old mentor, The Ancient One, was healing my wounded heart and soul. I kept on praying for understanding and guidance, and the messages from Beyond continued to come through. I was still active in the ministry and needless to say, many of my discourses were on the phenomenon of life and death.

Today, as I put these things in manuscript form, the grief is gone. I feel so privileged to have had the experiences, and the opportunity to share them with so many. I rejoice in the great freedom James has found, and celebrate my own release from fear of death and the great Unknown. I do not yearn for the Heavenly realms beyond, for my new awareness has taught me to enjoy and savor all of the life experiences that come my way while still here on earth. As the old adage goes "Heaven can wait".

Letters from Summerland

Principal Characters

The Spirit World

Radha   The Master Teacher in charge of James' spiritual growth in Summerland Radha, also, is able to guide Marian, due to the identical soul patterns of James and Marian.

The Lady   James' personal "tour guide".

Amaria   A counselor for the new arrivals in Summerland.

Clarence   A counselor for the new arrivals in Summerland.

Bruce   Marian's son, Lianne's husband, and father of Alisha and Phillip. A "fallen warrior" from the Vietnam war, he was a guitarist, singer, carpenter and mystic.

Troy   Marian's first husband. James, before he died, promised to "look him up" and try to help him if he could.

Grady   Father of Troy.

Brad   Friend of James.

North Carolina

Lianne   Widow of Bruce, James' friend and confidante; co-founder of Terra Nova Center.

Phillip   Son of Bruce and Lianne.

Alisha   Daughter of Bruce and Lianne.

Virginia   Close friend and church leader.

New Mexico

Tu Moonwalker   White mountain Apache Medicine woman, elder, Master Shamanic teacher, leader, healer, writer and artist.

Lané Sáan   Yaqui Medicine woman, elder, healer teacher and artist, associate of Tu.

Kay Thomas   Mutual friend of James and Marian.

Mary-Margaret   Channel for the Bartholomew teachings.

Josseph Rynear   Internationally known astrologer, writer, teacher and mystic in Taos N.M.

Alice Rynear   Teacher, writer and mystic, wife of Josseph.

Cynthia   A close friend and therapist for James when he lived in New Mexico.

Marian: *It was well past my usual bedtime. I'd been sitting at my desk, trying to answer some of the letters I had received after James had died. My mind was filled with so many unanswered questions.*

What if it had all been just a dream? Where is James? Is he lost to me forever? Is he happy? Has he seen Bruce?

Suddenly I felt his presence all around me. It felt soft and comforting. I "heard" his voice in my head, saying "pick up the pen, Marian...write, write." Almost in a trance I pulled out a yellow pad and picked up the pen. Suddenly my hand began to write rapidly, nearly out of my control. I heard him say in my head, "Relax...we can do this if you will just let me in."

The sentences tumbled off the pen, somewhat jumbled up and running together. I could feel his excitement as he realized communication was possible. Filled with assurance of his love, the words comforted, but at the same time, brought more confusion. (His first messages were a jumbled mixture of reassurance about his love and excitement at the realization it would be possible to communicate. It took a few times for them to come through in a more orderly fashion.)

James: No, I am not lost to you forever, for aren't you yet aware that we really never die? So many things I want to tell you, to comfort you, but you don't trust my essence enough to let me in.

I was with you in the restaurant, touching you, helping you to comfort Cynthia. I am exquisitely happy, it's so beautiful and joyous here, even more than you told me it would be. So many friends and family, I've seen them all, what a wonderful reunion! I hold you in my heart now even as I did when I was with you. Didn't you say love never dies? You gave me the greatest gift of all, unconditional love, as did our dear family. Then, you knew our love was real, why do you doubt me now? I am a heart beat away, and constantly near you. I am with you in dreamtime, but you cut our time short by your sporadic sleep patterns. I pledged my love forever and ever, don't you know that I meant it? Even as you write, my hand is on your shoulders.

Thank you for helping me to understand and for loving me, even when I was confused. You made my journey soft, and sweet and gentle. I pledge to do the same for you when the time is right.

So much work yet for you to do, I will help every way I can. Take good care of yourself, we need you and your body in good health to complete what we've set out to do.

I've searched for you for over three hundred years and I thank the blessed Creator that at last I found you again. *

When your mind rages with questions and doubts, you shut me out, and push me away. I need for you to believe I now live in you as part of our whole essence. Only in this belief can we complete our task. I've never stopped loving you, and now, as I see your beautiful spirit, my love is more than I could ever express while there with you physically. Let me in, for I need you to help me in this work. Please pick up the pen often. I think we will be able to communicate effectively this way. Please do not feel alone, I am really with you. Please don't beat yourself up with doubts and fears. I was real, our love was real. It didn't end, it has only just begun. No, it wasn't just a dream! It was the most real thing we both will ever experience.

By the way Bruce is fine, sends love and hugs. I see him often. He says you still don't take good enough care of yourself , He said, "Tell Doc to take it easy!" **

I've only gotten a glimpse of what may be possible if we do keep this fragile doorway open. Everyone that I've met over here has such a deep longing to communicate with those they left behind. Their frustration is the seemingly impossibility of letting their loved ones know *that they didn't die, and that they are allright*. I'm being eagerly encouraged to keep "hammering on the door", in the hope that *you* will be willing to "carry the message" that there is no such thing as death!

That is all for now, for I sense your disbelief and you are more than a little tired. Think about what I have said, and *please*, let me communicate this way often, not just for you and me, but for *everyone* who grieves.

James

Marian: *Not really believing it was possible, I sat in prayer and summoned James in my mind. In just a moment I again felt his presence, and asked him, is this a convenient time to write? (At this point I had told no one that these letters were happening.)*

James: Beloved one, it is always a convenient time to speak with you, for I will not be departing from you unless you send me away. Only you can close the door.

I know you want to know about the day of my "death". It was more beautiful than my mere words can describe. I heard your voice and felt surrounded by the love of all of you, then a slight "tug" and in an instant I was above all of you, accompanied by Bruce and several beautiful angel-beings. I knew the family wasn't yet aware that I had left the body and I was deeply touched by their tender touch and their tears. I saw your shock as the realization that I had "died" hit you. How I longed to scream "I'm right here!", but I didn't yet have power enough to materialize my form or my thoughts. I heard you ask to be left alone, and as the family left the room, I suddenly was whisked away, too.

Next, I was in a joyous, lovely place surrounded by a lot of family and friends, all trying to touch me and welcome me home. I wanted to rush back to you, but I couldn't get my body moving. A lady near me said my vital force hadn't yet been activated, but not to worry because they had guardians with me and that you would be all right. For a moment I felt kind of an anxiety, afraid I'd lost you, then I heard a voice near me say, "not so, she is part of you, rest now, soon you will see her."

Bruce kept grinning at me and said, "Hey man, that's quite a trip, isn't it? Welcome to heaven, or whatever they call it here, anyway, man I'm glad to see you face to face. I never doubted Mom would come through and get you safely across. It's beautiful, isn't it"? My four brothers were all talking at once, and one of my New Mexico friends who had died a while back came up, a bit bewildered and seemed amazed to see me there. I kept wondering about you and the family, so the lady told me to come with her. In a second, I was on the porch and I saw them wheel my body out the door. I felt anxiety for you and immediately was by your side in front of the mantle. I put my arms around you, but your grief was so great you couldn't feel me. I felt sad, because you were sad and I felt like crying. Immediately the lady said we had to go. In a flash I was back with my friends and family and Bruce. I felt joy and exhilaration, but confused about what to do for you. I never wanted to hurt you. I started to feel weak and then someone said I needed to rest. I was assured by someone else that you and the family were all being taken care of. Then I slept.

I've wanted to share this, but your grief, and later your doubts, kept blocking me. My beloved one, I love you more than you can ever know until you are over here. What we shared while together is only the tip of the iceberg. Love here is so much more, but I don't yet know how to describe it.

Soon, I will be able to share what I'm doing, learning and becoming, so you can use it to help others. Right now I'm so thrilled I can finally "talk" to you that I just can't get over how much I love you, like I wrote in that card, "forever and forever".

There's much more that I felt and experienced that first day, but we will wait until our next "talk". The lady, who keeps close to me, like a guide, I guess, (I don't know her name yet), says these first transmissions may be tiring for you, so I shouldn't talk too long. She said, when you get used to this type of communication it will be much faster and easier on you. Until we speak again, I am.

James

Marian: The process of "tuning in" to the highly charged vibration that indicated James was present was still somewhat unsettling. I felt self-consious and somewhat timid. My ability to participate in an actual dialogue with someone in Spirit was still on shaky ground. I felt anything except secure and self confident. Usually able to speak clearly, fluently, my words now seemed childish and simple. In the very beginning James told me he couldn't override the Cosmic Law that one first must ask in order to receive.

Incrediably, whenever the "doorway" opened, I was transported beyound grief, and a feeling of well-being would last for hours after the transmission. During those hours of peace, I absolutely knew the messages were valid! But, as the peace faded, I would slip back into denial and my own sadness. I knew that I would really have to work on expanding my own awareness, and belief system if these messages were to have any impact. This "doorway" literally was stretching my conscious awareness to the limits of my ability to comprehend and understand!

When it was my "turn" to open the sessions by asking questions, I froze. My questions, in the beginning, were childish and , to me, they sounded very mundane. I really didn't know **what** to ask.

James, what do you do over there? Where, or how do you live? Were you with us at dinner tomight? (Kay Thomas and I had a lovely time with two mutual friends, and of course, James, was the topic of conversation).

James: It was indeed, a lovely evening and I most certainly did accept your invitation to come along. You were right, I didn't have to pick up the check! You and Kay looked lovely and your friends are delightful.

You have no idea how wonderful it is to hear you laugh, and when you shared our love and life with Rose and Genie, it made me happy that your memories were so pleasant! We did have a grand time, while it lasted, didn't we? But, the very best is yet to come!

I'm in a sort of class now. You know I asked to be allowed to work with the family and you. Well, that isn't just a simple matter, it seems. I'm being trained by several teachers to communicate by thought transference. Lianne picked up my thoughts several times today, and once Alisha looked up abruptly, just like she could see me. My teachers are more like friends instead of guides and they are very loving and patient with me. I call one *Amaria* and the other is *Clarence*. Delightful people.

I didn't see Bruce today. He's really busy but I don't yet know what he does. I got to hear him play guitar and sing a short time ago. You were right, he does have talent. He said he's sorry he didn't share his music more with others while he was in your dimension.

I live in a lovely small country cottage with lots of roses and a quiet little brook running through the garden. I live alone, by my choice, but I don't feel lonely at all. I listen to beautiful music, read, and I'm trying my hand at painting! Surprise! I've got a bit of talent! How about that?

I have difficulty feeling and experiencing time, it just doesn't seem to exist, yet I'm aware it is passing. So very much to learn here!

I know you don't completely trust these letters yet but tomorrow I'm going to try to send you a sign. In the meantime, close your eyes and think of me. Don't you see my eyes, looking straight at you?

Did you know love can build a lovely bridge that crosses from your physical world to the spirit world? Love opens the doorway always. If only people would believe this! They could be spared so much of the grief.

James

Marian: *A White feather was lying on the carpet when I woke up this morning. The sign James promised? I smiled as I picked it up, and then he seemed to be right there. Again, he said, "write". In the course of our dialogue, I asked him, when you say you can "see" people that you love, how do you see them? Do you see them as they physically appear or what? Can you share more about your new life?*

James: Seeing in this world is different than it is in yours. We see through the *feelings*, and view the *essence* of people. We don't see height, weight, color, age, etc. We see the goodness and love in the soul. That is why when love and tenderness are present, if we have a soul connection, then the veil dissolves and visual contact is possible. That is one of the reasons guileless, and pure souls, many times, can "see" beyond the veil. It is always *love* that opens the door. But dark feelings close it totally, and no contact is possible.

Now, I would like to share more about my new life here in this heaven world I call home now. I go to a sort of clinic every day, or what passes for a day here. You know, the cancer had diminished my vital force and energy, so I get a kind of therapy on a regular basis. I'm taken into a roundish room, with several others. There we are bathed in a radiation of soft, pulsating lights that usually makes me tingle all over. Each session leaves me refreshed and "lighter". I seem to be getting considerably younger in appearance. I no longer wear my glasses. I think the clinic is for the regeneration of etheric substance, but I'm not yet sure how it works. There is so much here that I don't understand, and each new experience fills me with awe and wonder.

I haven't been to the Hall of Memories yet, but I think it will be soon. Others tell me to be prepared to see my errors in judgment in my last embodiment. I'm not really looking forward to that, but I realize I can't continue to grow unless I learn from past mistakes. Here the desire to learn and grow is very intense. Everyone here is excited about becoming clearer channels of life and light!

By the way, I saw my parents. Joe* brought them for a visit. It was pleasant being with them, but they aren't in the same place that I am. They look peaceful, youthful and are far more tender than I can ever remember them being. Joe wants to re-embody, but I don't know how soon that will be. Mother works at some kind of school for new souls, but I didn't understand what Dad is doing. They weren't surprised to see me and they didn't seem to have regrets when it was time to leave. They were more like friends than family. All Joe could talk about is being born again, he's really excited that he might get to do it so soon.

Say, aren't you supposed to be resting? I could talk all night, but I don't think you should try it. Rest now, for tomorrow is another day. Remember, you must *ask* before I can answer, that is the Law. Eagerly I await the opportunity to try to answer your questions. Don't be afraid. Just *ask*.

James

---

*Joe, one of James' brothers who died years earlier.

Marian: *I had been feeling very badly physically and sleeping fit-fully. When sleep came, my dreams were nightmarish and frightening. I had received several more messages from James, and in a fit of rage, tore them into tiny pieces, declaring I would not be a part of this anymore. Afterwards I felt nauseated and weak, definitely "out of sorts".*

In desperation I called Tu Moonwalker and told her what was happening to me. I voiced my fear that something from Spirit was "trying to get me"...(fear, again!). She made arrangements for us to meet that day. She and Lané Saán, responded to my complaint that "I felt like I had a knife in my back" by quickly "removing" one! It seems I had been under a heavy psychic attack from a jealous, angry friend, and her vicious thoughts were exactly like a knife thrust! (Words can hurt, even from great distances).

A beautiful healing session was held there on the New Mexico desert, and immediately I felt light and peaceful. When James again entered my thoughts, I couldn't think of anything to ask him, so I "opened" the door by asking if he knew about the healing session with Tu and Lané Sáan.

James: My beloved Marian. Amazing! Our dear Tu got to the bottom of your emotional disturbance in a matter of minutes! What you feel right now is pure grief, understandably so, but is no longer contaminated with a death wish. You are so sensitive that when someone projects intense anger toward you, it literally assaults you on every level. Couple such an attack with deep grief, and the desire to live begins to fade. Thank God, someone came to the rescue before things went too far! Please send my eternal love and gratitude to our dear Tu for helping me to take care of you.

I'm told you will need several days of rest to recuperate, so I won't press you tonight to write for me. In a few days we will resume the messages from my world to yours.

I heard Mike say the bear is helping dear Sean, and that he sleeps with it every night. That allows me to comfort him and talk to him behind sleep at night. (note: James gave Marian a clear impression to give his old teddy bear to Sean, a seven year old friend who was having a difficult time dealing with his death.) You realize, of course, Sean and I are old, old, friends. We have fascinating discussions when he "visits" me at night. He really scolded me for "leaving" you, and making you cry. You've got quite a little defender there!

I just saw Bruce, and he's happy about the new tractor. He said I should ask you why you didn't get that "play pretty" while he was there to play with it? He said he hitched a ride today with Jerry, and took a few spins around the field with him. He tried to tickle Jerry and get his attention, but Jerry would just brush away the sensation and kept on rolling along. First thing we know, Bruce will come riding up on a brand new John Deere tractor, for he can manifest as good as I can, I'm sure.

Also I've been thinking about the new CD player and all of the wonderful classical music you bought me. Nothing has happened yet, but I am trying to manifest them over here. It's the first time I've tried to create something that big. I'll let you know how it turns out. I have managed hot fudge sundaes, now lets see what I can do next

Tell my darling Alisha that I love her new haircut. I think all you ladies should have easy to care for hairstyles. And yes, I think she should have the doll she's asked for, for Christmas. I'm all for spoiling her and Bruce is right here egging me on. She's the one I wish I could comfort and reassure. (The only time I see Bruce really "down" is when he sees what our deaths have done to her. How we both wish she could have been spared such grief and pain).

Bruce had dinner with me tonight and he played guitar for a while afterwards. In a few minutes, we're going to visit Troy and Brad, and Bruce is taking along the guitar to play for them. He tried to show me a few chords, but I was all thumbs. A long time ago I thought I might like to be a guitarist, but obviously it's not my forte. Bruce said he misses his "grits" but I think he's putting me on. He really loves to kid around. He's so happy-go-lucky, I find it hard to believe he was ever depressed enough to commit suicide! He makes everyone laugh and everyone over here likes him.

Now it really is time for you to get some rest isn't it? I am so very excited about our ability to communicate this way! So many of my new found friends here are as excited as I am, because they all hope their own loved ones will hear about this, and thus some of their pain will be alleviated. After every transmission we sit around and discuss what was communicated. They would all like me to send messages for them, but my teacher tells me that is not the purpose of these sessions and to do so would interfere with too many individual karmic patterns. So, as the old saying goes, for right now it's just "you and me" kid.

James

Marian: Lianne had valiantly been trying to *"hold me together"* while I'd been going through all the inner turmoil over the letters. She encouraged me to keep writing and just *"wait and see"*.

In ceremony, both Lianne and I were *"adopted"* by Tu Moon-walker, our shamanic friend and mentor in New Mexico. I *"asked"* James if he knew about that, and I told him of Lianne's strong support.

James: Oh, Lianne! What a gem she is! If I had to leave I couldn't have left you in better hands. I was overjoyed when Tu asked her to be a kinsperson, a very great honor, long over due. She understands your unique, and often, fragile position in that body and will always be a barrier between you and that which would harm you. She is to you what Lané Saán is to our beloved Tu. She picks up my thoughts very easily whenever I am near her. As you know, I was married to her in a pioneer time, in the Ohio Valley. We cut our way out of a wilderness. She was a trooper then, just as she is now. A real trail blazer! I love her dearly. What a wonderful friend she was to me!

Last night when you invoked the Guardian Angels to surround you all in light, I could actually "see" a shield of shimmery, golden light around the property. Kind of like a cosmic M & M shell, don't you think? It certainly was proof positive that "ask and it shall be given". I always wanted to be able to see some of the things you could see, and now, I just seem to be able to see everything...backwards, forward, up, down, and even into the heart of things, like inside out! Whatever I think about just seems to pop into view. Even stranger, I somehow know *why* things look the way they do, and what people *really* feel, not just forming opinions based on words. Isn't it wild? Too bad we forget how to do this when we embody...it might eliminate the very human tendency to lie!

Today I "saw" Alisha acting sassy toward her mother, but I knew her heart was screaming for love and understanding. Do you suppose most of the people screaming and yelling at each other are, in reality, pleading for love? (Don't answer that, I already know your answer). Haven't I heard you say so many, many times that if we "listened with our heart instead of our ego, we wouldn't get so mad at one another?" Anyway, I just wanted to say I think I really am beginning to "see with my heart".

By the way, every time we communicate I am actually standing right beside you. In talking to others over here, I've discovered that *when there is a bond of love*, the one in the spirit world can, and *does* travel freely to the bereaved ones left behind. If only people could understand how close the ties that bind really are then perhaps the terrible sense of abandonment would be gone. O, that people could understand that when they *think* about their loved one, it *usually* means that the loved one is right beside them! If only they could understand that love is never lost. It is the one thing in this magnificent universe that really is forever! Love, I am finding out, really *is* the language of the soul!

James

Marian: I "told" James about having dinner with Tu and Lané Saán, and that I really felt his presence with us. I also, asked him about what kind of information he would be trying to send through me. And I was wondering about locale, where exactly, was James at this time. I had so many questions, especially about the Angels, what were they really like.

James: Well, tonight was delightful! I just sat back and basked in the love and comaraderie. I actually sat between you and Tu. Tu was in fine form, wasn't she? The love between you two warms my soul. I feel I've left you in very good hands.

The Lady told me I won't be sending higher teachings until I've completed my realignment with Source, which is what is actually happening in what I call the "clinic". I feel like that will happen very soon because my light "therapist" said earlier that I would soon be finished. In the meantime, I'll fill you in as much as I can on whats happening now.

You realize, of course, I've not left for another place. That, in actuality, I'm still present in the same "place" you are, just on a higher *frequency*. Sometimes, I can actually "see" you and the others that I loved, but most of the time, I sense and "feel" their essence. I'm always just a thought away, as close as a heartbeat.

We can duplicate favorite things here in this vibration. They are just as vibrant, and solid, as they are in your realm. Our bodies feel light and free of pain, but they have actual substance and density...in fact, if it weren't for the incredible sense of freedom and joy I would feel just the same as I did before I "died". I've got the same solidarity now that I had then and I'm still "James" in every way.

We don't see angels here, as we have been led to believe the way angels *should* be. But, there are many exceptionally beautiful, shining, radiant beings that I suspect are really angels. Everyone here is so cooperative, loving, and friendly. I've heard that you must *earn* the right to be here, and that if you are angry, resentful or fearful, you can't be here.

So, there is no discord here at all.   I really feel the heaviness and pain where Brad and Troy are. So much sadness there. I can't go there alone without the Lady. I think she protects me while I'm there. She doesn't ever speak or interfere, but if the vibrations begin to feel "heavy", I feel her enfolding me in a soft blanket of loving energy that tends to strengthen me. Then I'm able to continue to talk to them, without being diminished. She said she wants me to learn how to do this for myself, but for now it is part of her assignment.

I really want to be a counselor and friend that can help out in that Grey area*. There are some very fine souls "stuck" there just because they were never told of higher things. I've seen so much grief and pain and fear in that place! How I long to try to help them break free and rise up to the higher, more beautiful plane that I now live in.

Did you feel my kiss tonight in the car? I felt like you did, because your hand went immediately to your cheek. I think you and I are being re-aligned so that we will be able to bridge from the Known to the Unknown. I'm amazed at how clearly you now receive me.

I'm so happy Tu finally convinced you that these letters are really from me. With Bart and Tu both endorsing them, do you think you can now set aside your fears and reluctance to write? It is wonderful to communicate with you tonight, since your fear seems to be gone. I'll be happy to hear Josseph Rynear's comments. I think he tunes to my frequency very easily.

By the way, I'll travel with you and Kay to Taos tomorrow. The Lady said I don't have class or clinic, and I'm free. I know you plan to pray for me at Chimajo. I'll be right beside you while you do this, but, please, don't let that stop you! We all need all of the prayers we can get! Always!

There is concern here that you "run" on raw nerves, and don't get enough actual sleep. As we bond even closer, and your sense of loss diminishes, I hope you will rectify this soon!

I feel your tiredness and now you're missing part of the transmission. I have found that when physical tiredness or sadness overcomes you, the communication becomes very "spotty" and that our minds aren't synchronized enough to make a connection. A note I might add, is that anyone longing to "connect" with a departed loved one must do so from a balanced and loving place. Unless the seeker is rested, peaceful and quiet, connection is not possible. It is only in harmony and stillness that spiritual communication is ever possible. Tomorrow then?

James

---

* The Grey Area is actually part of the Bardo where souls who have much human error and karma go upon leaving the body. There they rest, heal and study until time to return to the earth in another body.

Marian: *Kay and I were driving the back road from Albuqurque to Taos, N.M.   This narrow and winding road had towering cliffs on one side and a 700 foot drop on the other.   We had seen no traffic at all when suddenly a black sedan driven by a dark haired woman careened around a curve, headed straight for us.*

"O, God, help us!!" I screamed, as Kay fought to get out of her way.   As suddenly as the car appeared it was gone!   We pulled over, stopped and tried to stop shaking.   Looking down the road, the black car was nowhere in sight!   We prayed, giving thanks to our angels of protection and although badly shaken, continued on our way.   Thank God for angel protectors

For several days I had been concerned about family and financial matters.   It seemed like everyone I talked to was in trouble and I was confused about what I was supposed to do about it.   When James "arrived" I was still feeling frustration.   I had no particular questions but was just "open" to whatever he felt like sharing.   I did, however, ask him about the encounter on the road to Taos.

James: That was a close call on the road today! You *must* keep all shields intact at all times. Be aware forces of evil would like to remove you from the plane of activity for the Light! I am powerless to do this for you. Sometimes you take protection very lightly, you know. But, I'm not here to lecture you, I only want you to be safe.

Are you aware that when you allow yourself to get upset, you shut the door of communication between us? As I told you earlier, no discord can exist on this plane; any negative emotion or words "slam" an invisible door between us. When are you going to quit beating yourself up over things that aren't your problem? You are not the caretaker of the world. You don't have to "fix" everything for everyone; do you understand, my love? Did you not, yourself, say each person must learn and grow for themselves? That no one else has the right to try to help them avoid life's very valuable lessons? But, enough said, I think in your heart you know what I want you to do. Look out for yourself for a change. Lighten your burdens. Enjoy and take care of you.

The "good news" is I'm sensing greater compassion and humility in my consciousness lately. Nearly everything touches my heart and brings tears of joy to my eyes. I was afraid I was becomeing a "basket-case", but the Lady assures me I am having very natural reactions. She said my heart center was already opened before I arrived, so I am able to "feel" the beauty, peace, light and radiant joy! The more I feel the more I want to return to the grey place and get Brad and Troy out of there! It is so sad where they are.

Thank you for lighting the candles for Troy, Bruce and myself to-day at Chimajo. Please, light one for my friend Brad. He really needs much prayer and Light. I've noticed that every time someone there sends prayers and Light, it gets softer and lighter in the grey place. *Send more light!* Maybe we can effect a massive rescue action. So many fine souls are "stuck" there. I just want so badly to help them, now that I've seen what they can really aspire to reach.

I've been working on learning to manifest over here. What great fun! By the way, I got a CD player and discs a few days ago. Mine is *exactly* like yours and just for fun, I got a Jim Reeves tape. Would you say I'm mellowing a bit?

The experience today shattered your auric field. I'm told that I should not force you to keep communication lines open tonight. I feel you should go to bed and get a good night's sleep. I'll be right there with you, looking out for you as always. Say, that's another strange phenomena, I am here with you in New Mexico, but I just watched Alisha working on a crafts project in the dining room in North Carolina, both at the same time! Now, I wonder how *that* works?

(Marian had talked with Josseph in Taos, N.M. and he urged her to continue the writing. He felt the letters had great validity). Thank   God,

Josseph and Alice feel good about these letters! I know how much you value their opinions. I just want you completely free of any doubts or fears. One thing I've finally realized is how much we, as humans, need others to validate us. In class that was discussed, and the need to teach children early on to believe in themselves and have self-esteem. It was also brought out that we, whether embodied here or there, aren't isolated "islands" and we really do *need* one another. So, *trust* issues are a major part of humanity's Homeward journey. Remember, trust in the Creator, yourself and in one another.

James

Marian: *Today I met with Mary-Margaret Moore, the channel for Bartholomew, and received a wonderful healing hug from her. We both felt the presence of "Bart" and James, so we called it a four way hug. Earlier I had given a public talk and many of our mutual friends gathered around afterwards to offer condolences and comfort over the death of my husband.*

Several people mentioned that they felt the presence of many angels during the meeting. Deep inside I just knew those "angels" were James and his friends, as well as various spiritual guides and teachers.

James: Well, Bart has done it again! Another wonderful "four way hug", I didn't want it to end. When you put your head on Mary-Margarets shoulder, it was me that was holding you. Bart merged with my essence, and Mary-Margaret with yours, and those few minutes of deep embrace were balm to my soul. What made me happiest was that you knew and accepted what was happening. Precious moments, indeed!

Your talk this morning was inspiring as always. A fairly large group of us attended just to hear you. Everyone, afterwards, was excited that Truth is being taught on your plane. As always, I was very, very proud of you.

Say, I forgot to ask how you liked the white feather that I sent you? I thought you would recognize White Hawks signature card. Neat, isn't it? It is strange how these things work. I just concentrate, and it appears. And when I want to send you more, invariably a receptive mind of some one who loves you picks up the thought and acts on it. Even your friend Morgan "heard" my desire to give you a gift, bingo! Earrings! (Marian told Josseph and Alice love must be what makes these things happen).

You've got it, the key is love. I can't inspire anyone to act like a messenger unless there *is* love. As often as feasible, I will send my "calling cards" just so you will know that I am still with you.

When you reached out to touch so many people at today's gathering, several of us grabbed the opportunity to amplify the energies by merging with yours. There are going to be some very surprised people tomorrow, when they find much of their grief and pain is gone. Someday this will be a natural order of things; right now it's still "cosmic high-jinx". When the veil of fear has been dissolved, people from many different planes will work freely together in *teamwork*, balanced in perfect love and understanding. As long as man doesn't recognize his/her self as spirit, it will remain a hit and miss action. So, it will be called "miracle", when in actuality, it is divine order at work. A very natural blending of above and below!

Go and rest now, we will talk again soon.

James

Marian: *James, after the clinic work and The Hall of Memories, what lies ahead for you in your new life? What is your work or duties over there?*

James: Service, *always service.* That is the motto for everyone here. New arrivals quickly pick up the joy of being able to help others. Everyone works, if you can really call it such, to get balanced and energetically fit, in order to play a productive role.

We are so enfolded in the serenity and joy, our souls long to help others find the same thing. The very Essence of the Christ permeates all. There are no third dimensional words to try to tell you what it is like. The peace and love fills us to overflowing; not even a flash of darkness or fear can be found here.

Marian: *Is the service to those still embodied in human form, or is it just in your world or other parts of the spirit realm? What do you do?*

James: It is both. Many here act as Guardian Spirits for people on earth. Some, like myself, have been given permission to work in the Gray area. That is where I go to talk to Troy, Grady and Brad. As they learn, and want to move upward, they will be able to leave there for a higher plane. Love is the only way, so I talk to them a lot about forgiveness and love. I have chosen this work, which hardly seems like work at all. It is so deeply rewarding for me personally.

My other "mission" is to work with you to try to teach that there is no death, only Life ever expanding, changing. Again I *volunteered* to do this. There aren't any "bosses". Everyone just seems to know what needs to be done and they do it.

As for the future, I've no idea at this point in what we laughingly call time. I dwell now in a veritable paradise, yet, I've been made aware that there is much, much more beyond this place. At this time my poor earthman's consciousness can't even begin to comprehend a world greater than here!

Many here, like the Lady, act as escorts and guides for the new arrivals. (Remember I'm still the new kid on the block over here). The Escorts never interfere; but they stand by in case the neophyte oversteps their present ability to remain centered. They may suggest, but never insist their assignee do any particular thing. Whenever I'm in doubt, the Lady instantly appears. How do you suppose *that* works?

Clarance and Amaria also are in escort work. They, literally, are part of the *Welcoming Committee*. When a soul comes over here that is one of the first jobs available to the new arrival. Those with strong emotional ties to loved ones still embodied will *usually* volunteer for *Welcoming* just in case one of their loved ones crosses over. They want to be there to greet them. There are many truly great teachers (or Masters), but I think one would have to be here a long, long time, and gain great wisdoms in order to become one.

I've met several here who volunteered to be a Guardian for a child or friend still on the earth. That way they are able to be involved as the loved one continues to grow. You know, we always talked about our *"Guardian Angels"*, but it appears people just like me can be one, and I'm certainly not an angel! Maybe the term *"Guardian Spirit"* would be more accurate. Now don't take that as gospel truth; I'm just making an observation. There's just so much to learn yet.

Be at peace, until next we talk.

James

Marian: *I experienced another bout of grief mixed with my home-sickness for North Carolina. In my rage and hurt I questioned everything; including these communications. As the stress poured out, everything in my life seemed to be falling apart. When the tears were spent, I prayed with Alice Rynear, and a beautiful calm, peace enfolded me. I told her, "You know, I don't even know where James is". She was quiet for a moment, and then softly said, "Why, Marian, he's in* **Summerland***. I'm sure of it. Ask him". Somehow knowing a name really seemed to help, and then I felt the quiet calm that meant James was near. Picking up the pen, I asked him if he really was in a place called Summerland.*

James: Well, the "storm" has passed, and you're settling down into your usual sweet self. Do you feel better now, about me, the children, money, life and protection? You certainly covered the whole spectrum today, didn't you?

Oh, I was overjoyed to hear Alice name this place! When she said *"Summerland"* thrills and tingles ran up and down my body! Even Bruce didn't seem to know what it is called, and no one else volunteered anything except "Here". I love the name *"Summerland"*, it has a grand ring to it! You know me, I like to know where, why and what's it called.

I feel so powerless when you get upset, because I can't help you. I can only stand by until the turmoil passes. The Lady talked to me a bit about you. The shamanic work with Tu, your own channeling, and now trying to attune your self to my frequency, all on top of your grief, has been traumatic for you in many ways. So much is being asked of you in such a short time. It is no wonder you question your sanity. But, my beloved, you are one of the sanest of the sane. So, please don't be hard on yourself. Even the cells of your body are in a changing mode, and I shudder to think of the beating your emotional body is taking! All of this is necessary in order to allow us to play our part in the emergence of Truth and peace on the earth plane. I don't know yet exactly what your role is, or mine for that matter. But this much I have discovered, there are those here who consider this work very important to the over-all plan! You have no idea how proud that makes me. But, then I was always awed by you, and very, very proud of your work.

I'm not going to write long. It's been such a stressful day for you. I just have to be sure you are all right. I'll really be near you tonight. Since our soul fusion*, I'm with you most of the time. Rest well my love, tomorrow is another day.

James

* The soul fussion he speaks of is the mystical marriage, or melding of the masculine and feminine aspects of twin souls finally reunited, James and Marian are twin souls.

Marian: _I had no particular questions for James. I was tired from the tour, and sitting quietly in a meditative state. As always he was in my thoughts, and almost absent mindedly I picked up the pen and started to write. Then I felt the soft, loving essence of his presence, and the words flowed onto the paper effortlessly._

James: My beloved, another pleasant day for you, passing without tears. I so hope these communications are a healing for you. You have no idea how your grief tears me apart. You, whom I've loved completely and wholly, should not have to bear such sorrow because of me. (No, I'm not falling into guilt, I just don't want you to hurt).

In class today we were taught that we have reached the point of no return, and that each of us are aspiring toward union with Christ. When the question was asked if we would be returning to earth, our teacher said, _"No, beloved ones. Your path leads upward to more heavenly realms. Your earthly service now will be as guides and guardians. And only if you insist, will you return to form and matter. Your work will be on the planes beyond the earth, and your journey is onward and upward until you re-unite in God. Have no fear of loss, for your twin flames will continue to grow until they, at last, unite once more with you."_

Her eyes penetrated my very soul, and I knew, without speaking, she was answering my question about you. As if in answer to my seeking, she continued in her soft, melodic voice. _"Each one of you have fused, or joined, through your essence with your Twin Souls. Even though your cosmic mates remain embodied, you can never again be lost from them. You will be learning how to "bridge" the dimensions of spirit and matter in order to create an outpouring of knowledge to the third dimensional world. There are many still embodied who are, for the most part, impris-oned by their fear of dying. To this end we are seeking to open your com-munication powers. And as you learn, you will quite freely communicate and visit with your mates"._

There are only four of us, all males, in this particular class, and oddly enough, we each have a soul partner still on earth. I could feel the surge of joy that rippled through the class, as the realization of what she was telling us began to "sink in". I think we are going to be learning some very valuable things in the near future. I feel so privileged to have gotten this far. And now, to be told I won't lose you again, is beyond my mere words of expression.

My teacher, who's name is *Arielle*, said I can stand next to you in your lectures and "prompt" you, if necessary, to allow far greater truths to be channeled. It is wonderful to know we are going to be allowed to work together. You know, our dream was to be partners in Truth! It's almost like my dreams and visions are coming true, right now.

I wish you could see me, darling girl. I'm stronger now, and the lines have left my face. I feel vibrant and alive and I think I will finally regress, if that is the correct word, to about the way I was at 42. Maturity, understanding and health, to this end I continue my clinic work. Now I go to a second clinic, where I'm being raised, through *sacred sounds and Light*. After each treatment I feel like I'm so much more aware than ever before. And a peace that defies description floods my being!

There's certainly no wasted time here, and I stay very busy. But I still have much quiet time at home, working in my garden and painting. And, always my music. I've tried to paint you, but all I got on my canvas was radiations of Light and your beautiful eyes. I don't think portraits are my greatest talent. Right now I'm working on a painting of the Sandia Mountains*. I get excited or at least, exhilarated, each time I feel the electro-magnetic current run through my body. It always means it's time to write through you again.

(Note: Andrea, a mutual friend, had returned from Peru and Marian felt a strong urge to give her a ring, and make plans for dinner the following evening).

I won't be with you and our dear Andrea tonight. There's another concert and I really don't want to pass it up. I've never loved you more than when you gave her the ring from both of us, exactly what I wanted you to do.

Please tell dear Josseph to "lighten up", so much stress isn't doing him much good and I'd hate to see him over here before his time. Alice is a delight, isn't she? I always think of her surrounded by flowers.

My love, I'll let you go for now. We'll meet again later. Have a glorious time tomorrow as you explore your **outlaw trails. Who knows, I may go with you. Enjoy your time together for there are tremendous changes ahead for you and dear Ellen***. This may even be your last chance to "run away" on one of your exploration adventures.

James

* The Sandia Mountains are in New Mexico, near Albuquerque. James lived many years at Cedar Crest, in the Sandias.
** Marian and a friend planned a day trip to Cimarron to retrace part of the old outlaw trails.
*** Ellen, a dear friend, was taken ill and passed from this world two years later. It was indeed, the last trip we were to make together.

Marian: *Upon my return to North Carolina I felt washed out and subdued. On the second day home I again "felt" James's presence and picked up the pen to write. I relaxed and felt my thoughts wander, reaching out to him. I asked him more about the Grey zone and how Troy was coming along.*

James: My beloved, it warms my soul to see you settling into a comfortable frame of mind in order to receive these communications. How blessed we are. Truly, death had no sting, for we have never parted. I am closer to you now than I was while embodied, for we join together in essence. Last night, I at last knew you accepted my nearness, and you were comforted by it.

I'm spending much time in the Grey zone. A place of sorrows and despair. I want to be part of the rescue teams that go there to help lift those tangled in pain, up to a place of Light. Both, Brad and Troy seem glad to see me, and it thrills my soul as I see new ideas take root. All of my dreams of being a loving, caring male mentor are now becoming a reality.

I certainly understand now your reluctance to criticize Troy, in spite of the alcoholic violence that was experienced. I find him gentle and caring, even though he is remorseful, and guilt ridden. He still has much difficulty understanding God as spirit, and still thinks along the lines of a stern, judgmental personage that must punish him. How happy I will be when he realizes no one judges him but himself. He asks often if you hate him. I assure him you have only tenderness and love for him. Please continue to pray for him, for it greatly helps his awareness. It helps him to realize there is love for him. And, pray for me, thats a nice "deposit in my Grace account", to coin your own words.

The time is brief for you, so we will continue this later today.

James

51

Marian: *After dinner I sat at my desk re-reading all that had been recorded. I wondered what on earth I should do with all this information. Suddenly, I felt James very near, and again picked up the pen to write. I asked him to tell me more about his work over there.*

James: Hello again. I'd like to talk more about the Grey zone. You can see I'm really getting into my work. *If only people could realize that thought by thought they are creating their own hereafter!* Somehow, all people must be taught, from early childhood, how to create harmoniously! It is frustrating to find nice people over here enmeshed in fear, pain and self-created agonies. I pray you will teach more and more along these lines, helping people understand that they alone create their own destinies. Books have mentioned this, but far too little has actually been taught to turn mankind's thinking around. This *must* change! We, here in Summerland, can *attempt* rescue work, but the real solution lies there on your plane. It is in infancy that the examples and learning must begin. As souls evolve, consciously trying to live harmoniously and gratefully, all planes will progress, and the grey areas will begin to empty out. Please, won't you help us in this endeavor?

I know it seems like I spend all my time in the Grey area, but, that is not truth. I speak a great deal about it, because I've chosen it for my "calling", and I need your help, my love. My "days", if that be what they are called, are filled and joyous beyond words. I love my class work, and clinic has become a great pleasure. I saw my face reflected in the stream this dawning, and was amazed at the beauty and serenity reflecting back to me. I've seen the beauty and light of others, but I was pleasantly surprised to know that I am radiant, also.

I can't begin to tell you how close we are, you and I. The soul fusion has made us truly one.

Last night, in dreamtime*, you journeyed with me to visit my children. What a pleasant reunion we had. I wondered today, if dream memories carried over into their awakening? My heart wells up with love for them, as it does for all that I left behind. I was so happy to hear you tell Alice on the phone this morning that you knew we had been together. That is why you feel surges of energy and joy, instead of being weak and sad. How my very soul sings with joy, when you acknowledge my touch, hear my voice, or recognize my presence. Every day I grow more and more aware of what it means to be "truly one". Beyond mere words!

James

---

* While the physical body gets the rest it needs in sleeptime, the spirit is free to travel to many, many places in the universe. Often these "nighttime journeys" are spent with loved ones who have passed on. Hence, we often "dream" of a departed one, which usually isn't a dream at all, but an actual behind sleep visitation.

Marian: *Several weeks passed with only minor encounters. My feelings still felt like I was on a roller coaster. So many unanswered questions led me to ask James what he actually felt about our relationship now? I'm puzzled about desire and feelings between people who exist on different planes. Would you comment on this, please?*

James: I am also impelled to try to talk about desire on my side of the veil. When I am near you, and you are receptive to me, I *do* feel desire. A deep longing to merge with you overwhelms me, and generally, I am aware you feel the same. It isn't the "fire in the loins" desire felt on earth, but something much deeper. It is more like the soul's longing for completion. A longing that can only be fulfilled by union with one's other half. During those times I find myself speaking words of love, and touching you. Your grief is still fresh, so my out pourings often bring your tears. Yet, my need to be with you is far too strong to be ignored. When my desire for union comes, it is very powerful, and often frustrating because you aren't with me. The only difference is that it passes very quickly as I move my thoughts to something else.

Does this answer your question? I am getting stronger every day, and my joy grows by leaps and bounds! I never tire of looking at the incredible beauty of my surroundings. We don't have seasons here, so it is always fresh, green and bountiful. Flowers are beyond words to describe, their fragrance and beauty is almost intoxicating! Exhilarating! There are perfect crystal formations everywhere, as common as gravel is on earth. The sun strikes them and rainbow colors flash in all directions. Beautiful, breathtakinging colors!

I found a lovely woodland park today, and sat for a long time beside a sparkling waterfall. The songs of the birds were lovely! I felt as if I had somehow been led there for more healing, even though I was alone. (This was while you were in the mountains, I think). I was so content, I just didn't feel like rousing myself to go with you. I knew you were in good hands with your friends!

Marian, my beloved, I feel the strong urge to continue today's portion of our saga. Please, bear with me, and I'll try not to tire you out.

I heard the joy and laughter as you shared with your friends. It made me happy that it was a glad reunion, instead of mournful and sad. You have no idea how much you are teaching and inspiring others, as you *"set sail straight into the wind"* in your grief process! I like Tu's description of you as an exemplar, for your example teaches far more than words. When all Light workers become aware they must teach *by their own example*, rather than techniques and words, transformation of earth will be close at hand!

I'm so happy you are teaching about *neutralizing* powerful, angry words. Perhaps, if more people would shift into *neutral*, less psychic "garbage" would be spewed out and earth's healing could begin. One of my first "seminars" over here was about the damage being done by *thoughtless words*. I cringe when I recall things I said in ignorance and anger while embodied on earth. Fortunately, I was also shown "forgiveness and grace" so I don't carry remorse around in my soul. I simply recall, remember, review those actions and then release them. How I wish earthlings could do the same, then the past would truly become a great teacher.

I've not seen "Jesus", as we have all been taught we would when we reach "heaven". What I am beginning to comprehend is that the *personage* Jesus, was a Divine Pattern, into which each seeker must eventually be moulded. *Amaria* said, when questioned, that after I had totally healed, and reconnected with my own Divine Essence, I will be able to journey to higher planes where I will come face-to-face with Christ, Buddha and the Great Masters! I can't even begin to imagine a greater place than where I am now, but she said it was a thousand times more beautiful there. My poor head can't even imagine what it will be like!

Everyone here longs to be needed and to serve. Service is a way of life here in Summerland. I've made so many wonderful new friends. We often laugh about our "earthly trials and struggles", for here we know those things were simply illusions that helped us to grow. You can't even begin to imagine how liberated we all are feeling, just knowing none of the pain, grief, sorrow and fear was ever real!

I love my work as a mentor in the Gray area. Troy and Brad are my special "charges". They are learning to trust each other, and both of them seem to look forward to my visits. I'm still trying to explain "God", and also, the mechanics of death. At least, both of them are responding. (I might have mentioned earlier that Troy *has* been reunited with Grady, his father). The progress is slow, but the Light is beginning to filter in, and dissipate the gray shadows somewhat. Please, ask people to send Light to this sad plane. The Bardo, I think it's called. I see people wandering around there like lost souls, bewildered, hurt and guilt-ridden. It breaks my heart, when I realize what wonders await them in Summerland. Please, help me get them out of there! Light! More Light! Prayers! Love!

We are like a missionary action, operating with far too few tools. Please, ask all of your teachers and students to flood the Gray area with Love and Light! A vast rescue action is needed there. It would break your heart to see them wandering so hopelessly. I thank the Blessed Creator for teachers like you, Bunny, Cynthia and Bart for helping me correct my course. All of you helped me to by-pass the gray place, and get right straight into Summerland. The blessed love Lianne and you, with the family and friends gave to me, literally, set me free! How can I ever thank you, except by diligently working to help some one else break free?

I went looking for Troy because you asked me to. I was pleasantly surprised to find him sensitive and caring, so we are becoming fast friends. It doesn't seem strange at all that we both love you. It isn't a bit competitive. He understands you and I are true soul mates, and he's happy you learned to love again. He was afraid he had "killed" that within you by his abusive and unloving actions. He said you were always "a lovely woman, a good woman", but he just didn't know *how* to express love. He really wants to learn the things I learned in my years of counseling and therapy. I think when he returns to earth next, he will be much more caring and gentle than he's ever been before.

Brad is fighting his "sexual identity" battle. He doesn't trust or care for his feminine side, and he has a lot of bitterness over past hurts stemming from his recent sexual patterns. But, I am fond of both of my "charges", so I certainly won't give up on them.

I am told, as I work in Bardo, I am increasing my own Light! That is a comforting reward, indeed!

I found out Bruce is still "working" the Middle East war zones, in soul retrieval*. He also works with warriors who commit suicide, often greeting them when they cross over. Many Vietnam veterans are still arriving here by their own choice. I wish I could see more of him, because I certainly like him. He said he wished I played guitar, but I told him I thought I'd stick to painting for the time being. He speaks often and so lovingly about Lianne. But, he is willing for her to find a new life mate, for he knows that everyone needs love and companionship. Love here transcends the personal elements that are experienced on earth. In truth Love is *all* there is! Loving memories of oneness do live on, beyond the veil, for love is the *only* thing any of us can take with us as we leave the earth plane. All that is not love, like dirty garments, simply drops away and is left behind.

The lady just tapped me on the shoulder ever so lightly. I think she's indicating I'm tiring you, though I've so much I want to share. But tomorrow is another day, isn't it?

James

* Soul retrieval is when someone falls in battle, an act of conflict or terrorism. Spirit volunteers go to the battlefield to "escort" the shocked souls Home. In every war, thousands of spiritual guides hover close to the conflict to render assistance to those who are killed. No matter how fierce the battle, no one ever dies alone!

Marian: *We were preparing a special tree planting memorial service for James and for Bruce. Beautiful red maples had been purchased and the ground was being prepared. The following Saturday (weather permitting) James's ashes were to be taken to the mountains as he had requested. The interesting thing was I hadn't mentioned it to him, but he commented, anyway. That is another aspect of the mysteries surrounding our communications between worlds. I was feeling frustrated because every time we planned the ceremony the weather changed!*

James: I love the idea of the red maples being planted to honor Bruce and myself. Even to the fact that part of my ashes will be there. What a beautiful living tribute to both of us. I plan to be on the mountain Saturday when you throw my ashes to the wind. Wiseman's View, what an appropriate place,

For so long you have taught people how to live. Now, please, try to teach them how to die gracefully. I think you should write about the Garden of the Beloved and the Immortals. So many here are excited that we have a clear and open channel to help dispel the terrors of death and the unknown. The last great barrier between heaven and earth!

By the way, I've not seen my Grandmother or Karla. I'm sure they are both already back on earth. I have seen so many relatives and friends over here. I still look for Chief Chata-ti-ah*, but so far he hasn't come to me. Perhaps we will meet face-to-face after I've completed my healing on all levels.

James

* Chata-ti-ah was a spirit guide for James, who, also gave James the honorary name White Hawk.

Marian: *When the messages first started coming I made an effort to record dates and times, and keep them in a chronological order, but I finally gave that up. I received them in some of the strangest places, like flying over Oklahoma, in the gardens, at home, in the middle of the night, etc. There was no particular pattern as to the time or place. I often had nothing except deposit slips from my check book, an old envelope or a scrap of paper to write on. Consequently messages were recorded hastily on whatever was available, and later I would try to accurately transcribe them.*

On this day, I asked James what he thought about the red maples that are intended as a tribute to his memory and to the memory of Bruce.

James: The trees are absolutely beautiful. Living trees are such a wonderful tribute to anyone who has left the physical world. They will certainly give forth a glorious pallet of reds. By the way, who gets to rake up the leaves? I don't rake leaves! Neither does Bruce!

I heard you decide to cut out all of your local counseling at least until next year. A very wise decision, I think. You have no idea what a great toll these past few months have taken on your physical body. I just wish you could sleep more. Those few hours of weeping, tossing and turning each night are doing very little to heal your body or emotions.

I don't think you're "tuned in" to teaching tonight, so I'll just keep this simple. I told you of several new things that I've discovered, but my thoughts just didn't register with you. I think that is a good indication you are exhausted. Rest now and be at peace. Remember, we need you in a healthy body, to get our work done. All of this stress isn't helping much.

Tomorrow you take the ashes to Wiseman's View. Funny, but I feel no attachment at all. I just want to go along because the whole family will be on an outing, a fun day!

James

Marian: *Today the family and several close friends took James's ashes to the mountains to be scattered in the same place we had scattered Bruce's ashes two years earlier. It was a beautiful day, but windy and crisp. A funny thing happened when Alisha took her turn at tipping the urn. A sudden gust of wind blew the ashes back in her face and she yelled "Help! James is blowing all over me"! Little Sean solemnly closed his eyes and said a silent prayer when it was his turn. And, me? I started to cry. It just seemed so final!*

At one point the strong wind nearly knocked me off my feet, and our friend Larry, grabbed my hand to keep me from being pushed over the edge of the cliff.

The rest of the day went well, and we returned to Charlotte toward evening, I was curious about whether James had been with us on the mountain, so just before retiring, I sat for a few minutes in quiet contemplation, and immediately felt the soft, gentle energy of his presence. I asked him if he had been with us today.

James: Thank you for the lovely "send off" in the mountains. Yes, I was there. When the wind caught the ashes, I felt such a sense of liberation as I've never felt before. The children were precious, as they each took turns tipping the urn over. Dear Phillip, as he let the ashes go, I felt the depth of his love and pain for Bruce, also. I was so honored to be "liberated" at the exact place that my brother Bruce was. My heart was wrenched when your tears came. Your grief cut me to the depths of my being. You know how I said several here felt your courage, faith and "raw nerves" has kept you going? Well, I think the full scope of our separation "set in" there on the mountain. As the ashes flew away, I think some submerged hope that it was "just a dream" and you'd soon awaken, flew away, as well. When I saw the realization of the finality in your tormented eyes, I had to turn away. I simply couldn't bear to look into such naked grief.

I rejoined you and the family up on Grandfather Mountain, and was grateful Larry was there to take your hand. I was afraid that cold, fierce wind was going to blow you right off the mountain.

Tomorrow the tree ceremony will be held and Bruce and I will both be there to watch ourselves being so beautifully memorialized. May our trees provide shade and beauty for all who pass by, and a haven for the creatures of nature.

Thank you for giving dear Sean my old teddy bear for he really needs it. Bless his seven year old heart. He wanted so badly to heal me, and my passing hurt him deeply. The bear gives me a way to reach him, and comfort him. When I mentally suggested it, you picked it up at once, even telling Lianne he needed it much more than you did. Good girl. Together we, myself and brother bear, will try to fill up the emptiness in a special little boy's heart. Just like Alisha loves and uses her "James bear". (James, when he was ill, gave Alisha a teddy bear to hold whenever she thought about him).

I guess by now you realize my petition to be a "House Guardian" for the family and a "protector-teacher" for you has been granted. A glorious assignment of great love. So, I won't be leaving you ever again *unless* you push me away. Just reach out with your mind. You'll always find me waiting, open and receptive. Call it a reward for so many years of loving, selfless service. By the way, please tell others who grieve that their loved ones are *only a thought* away. If they could only *believe* we are all eternal spirit, grief would quickly turn to peace and joy. Spirit moves in and out of physical form, but it always *is*!

James

Marian: *Things were moving along peacefully, and most of the bouts of anger and denial seemed to be behind me. As I taught my classes, and did a limited number of counseling sessions, I often felt the gentle, encouraging presence of James. In my heart, I knew I wasn't alone.*

The red maple trees were finally planted, and a special memorial service held. I had done little writing in the past weeks. Instead, I was working a great deal on my emotional healing. Grief counseling was next on line for me, as I believed talking it out would speed up the healing process.

Sitting in the stillness, idly playing with the pen, I felt a soft touch, and knew James was near. There were no special questions in my mind, so I asked him how he liked the tree service. I also asked him to share more about his life in Summerland.

James: What a moment! The tree planting ceremony was a great event and Bruce was pleased that Laurie played his guitar. He thought it very touching when you placed a guitar pick and a crystal under his tree. He laughed when Lianne borrowed a cigarette to use the tobacco in a ceremonial way. He said it would have been fitting to put the whole pack in the hole. He said he really loved his "smokes". There was so much love from everyone, it deeply touched me. Sean, bless his heart, tried so hard to use the shovel. Thank all of our dear friends for their tribute to us.

I attended another special "seminar" to prepare me for the Hall of Memories. Many counselors were present and there were five, male and female, in our group. They talked to us about self-forgiveness and loving ourselves in spite of our over sights and mistakes. I sat in a special chair that had currents of energy running through it, in fact, all five of us had "chair treatment". It felt pleasant and stimulating. Radha, the leader, said it was to dissolve attachments to old energies, and to clear our force fields of self-condemnation and regrets. She said we needed to enter the Hall of Memories as clear and unencumbered as possible, and that was the purpose of the sessions. The only way I can describe it is that we emerged feeling "impersonal" and removed from the past.

Radha said these preparations are very necessary. If the souls weren't prepared in advance, their pain and guilt could cause them to experience a sort of insanity. Their grief would be more than they could bear. In the Memory Halls *everything* is recorded, values, motives, lies, deceptions, anger, fears, etc., *nothing* is left out. The Lady will go with me, but she will wait outside the viewing chamber, unable to enter with me. In my thoughts I said, "well, if it gets too rough, I'll just close my eyes". Quick as a flash Radha informed us that we would "see" with our inner (soul) vision, so there's no way to shut out the images. So much for short cuts!

She said the entire lifetime is shown in about twelve earth minutes, presented in major segments at a time. No one *has* to go to the Hall of Memories until they are ready. But you know me, anxious to get it over with! I just want to clear away all the past errors and get on with my new life.

Radha said we will feel remorse and pain when we emerge, but immediately will be taken to Restoration Clinic, where personal counselors will answer questions and help us evaluate the lessons learned. She said, like earthly child-birth pains, healing comes quickly here in Summerland. She said if self-condemnation is too severe, then we would be taken to a Healing Temple for an energy over-haul.

She said on the lower levels, like the Gray area, it is much, much worse for the viewers than it is here in Summerland. There is so much love, beauty and compassion here that I can't imagine being "lost" in pain for very long. I just want to get it over. I especially dread what I'll find in my youth and before my spiritual awakening.

Thank God, you were such a good teacher. I still remember you saying "None of us deliberately set out to screw up, in fact we usually are trying to do our best. Ignorance is the villian, not the individual". You taught me we were *just learning*, that life was only a class room filled with illusions, and that in our *souls* we were always *innocent and loved*. I pray I can "hold on" to that truth when I finally see and feel the full impact of this last embodiment.

Well, I will tell you about my trip to the Hall of Memories when it's over. I'm experiencing twinges of anxiety about it right now. (We even have a fruity drink that is an elixir of sorts that quickly stops anxiety and fear, so I'm going to have one right now!)

James

Marian: *For several days I worked hard in my office, trying to catch up paperwork and just had not felt the urge to write again.*

Late one night I got a phone call from a woman who was mad at "God, her family, her job and the government". Like a cesspool of negativity she poured it all out to me on the phone. At first I felt "used" by her thoughtlessness. But the "teacher" kicked in, and I kept my head, offering her alternative ways to look at her situations. After nearly an hour during which I simply refused to get pulled down into her darkness, we prayed together and she hung up.

Immediately I felt the by-now familiar gentle love enfold me, and I knew James was present. Laughingly, I asked him how did I do, in his estimation, in dealing with the troubled woman. I didn't really expect an answer, yet one came.

James: Bravo! I was present when the woman steeped in self pity spent nearly an hour trying to suck you into it, too. You were magnificent. Never losing your cool, and all the while planting seeds of love, joy and encouragement. You've come a long way, baby! It wasn't so very long ago she would have pushed all your buttons and irritated you. Not tonight! You just kept getting stronger and more emphatic, and she hung up the telephone with a great deal of good stuff to think about.

I've got to admit, several of us from over here were eavesdropping, quietly encouraging you to stand steadfast in your love and light. All of us join together in saying, "well done"! You told her you would send Light to her. With your permission, we would like to try to help you do so.

Surprise! Troy and Brad are coming along so rapidly. I'm told I soon can take them on a brief preview of Summerland. I think when they get a glimpse of what they can aspire to, they will really get fired up. Both of them are now aware of their guardian angels, and are about to make a real contact. Right now, only the Lady and myself are accepted by them.

I expect to go to the Hall of Memories anytime now. Please pray that I can face my mistakes and errors without losing it. I'm working hard in class to forgive the foolish things I did and said, during those years of unawareness. Even so, I don't look forward to actually viewing it all over again. It's the *only* shadow here in Summerland, the dread of the Hall of Memories. I've seen several radiantly happy people return from there sickly and despairing. They say it is the *only* judgment over here, when we each one must judge ourselves. And, there's no way to by-pass it.

That was a giant step for you the other day when you allowed Laurie to take Bruce's guitar for a few days. I held my breath, not sure you could let the "sacred icon" leave for awhile. She will take good care of it, I know, and her new song certainly added a great deal to the memorial ceremony.

You know as you get more and more involved in day to day living, you will have less and less time to write for me. But we *will* talk again very soon.

James

Marian: Up until this point I had not actually seen James, except for, in my mind's eye, seeing his eyes looking at me. (The way we "see" in a daydream). Over and over I had asked why, if I am clairvoyant, couldn't I see him. No answers come to that one. I continued to feel his essence and "hear" his voice, but I couldn't see him.

One afternoon, resting in the rocker in my room, half dozing and definitely not thinking about the world beyond, I was jarred abruptly into full awakening!

The CD player came on spontaneously! It had stopped and cut off about an hour before, and I was too lazy to get up and start it again. The music blared out, and my chair started rocking back and forth, even though I hadn't moved! I opened my eyes and there he stood! Not like a ghost, but solid, vibrant, smiling, alive!

I quickly closed my eyes tightly, put up the foot stool, and tried to force the chair to be still. But it kept on rocking. The music kept playing! Opening my eyes, he was still standing there, grinning from ear to ear. He said "Write".

I was so shocked and at the same time overjoyed, I was only able to record bits and pieces of what he was saying. I couldn't move out of the chair. It kept on moving.

He seemed as overwhelmed at the physical encounter as I was. It is hard, now, to remember which one of us was the most startled! Needless to say, the words tumbled out of both of us without sequence or deep meaning.

Later I found out both of us had moved unconsciously, toward each other, and since I was in a very relaxed, peaceful state we actually met "in the dimensional doorway". At that point I could "see" in his world, and he could "see" in mine. (It was like meeting at the border where you have a foot in two different countries). I was to find out this would be my one and only visual contact with James while in a waking state.

James: Angel girl, you *see* me! You *see* me, don't you? My God, how I've prayed this would happen, that you would actually "see" me. Now do you believe I will never leave you?

Do you feel the chair rocking? I'm doing it! Look at me! Feel the chair rocking! You're sitting absolutely still! It's *me* making the chair move! See, you can't stop the chair from moving, can you? It's me, James, I'm moving the chair. I'm here, look at me!

This *is* really happening. I am right here beside you. O, God! Look at me! I am looking at you. Feel the chair rocking, no matter how you try it won't stop.

It's me. I'm doing it. Now won't you believe I'm here? I love you, Marian. I've always loved you. I always will. You didn't lose me. You can't. I'm part of you forever. (I was so shocked I forgot to write). Write! Write! You finally "see" me! Now, do you believe this isn't a dream?

See, even when you put the foot stool up, you can't stop the chair moving! I'm right here beside you. God, I've just got to make you believe.

No more doubts! No more grief! No more loneliness! We're together again, if only for this moment, maybe now you'll believe it.

My energy charge is evaporating. I slip from your view, but not from your essence and your force field. We are one, forever!

James

Marian: *After the visual encounter I was literally shaking like a leaf. I stared at the jumbled up words on the paper and it didn't even seem to register. Then an amazing thing began to occur.*

*A strange sense of peace enfolded me, and I began to "make more sense" out of this whole death and dying business. I knew I had a long way to go on my journey towards personal healing, but my **faith** had just received a tremendous boost.*

*After he "faded from view" I could think of many things I wished I'd asked him, but told myself I'd do it the next time I saw him. I did not know there would not ever be a **next** time.*

Marian: I didn't hear from James for about a week. This break in our communications was due to the fact that I was experiencing rapid highs and lows following our visual contact. I hadn't spent any quality time in meditation and I was reluctant to tell anyone about what had happened. From such a high place of contact, I had " fallen back to earth", back into the sorrow that encompassed my life.

I remember once, as a child, I saw the Northern Lights and was overwhelmed with the miraculous beauty. And the very next day, I denied ever seeing them and called it a figment of my imagination! So it was with the visual contact with James, just another figment of my imagination? But, it was so real! And the music kept on playing! And the chair kept on rocking.

The old doubts were coming up and I wanted to be free of all of it. I was just so very, very tired. Finally I quieted my jumbled thoughts and entered into the quiet that usually "opened the doorway" to the spirit world. Immediately I felt his presence, and my questions came tumbling out like a torrent. Are you still near me? Why don't I "see" you? Was our love real? Is it all just a fantasy? Are we ever going to be together again? Why were you in my life? Was...is...this all some kind of weird joke, a "set up"?

James: Marian, my beloved. We were "sent" to help each other, because we are *parts* of the same whole. I know it seems like a dream because there was so little time, but it was real, and it *is* forever. Yes, we will be together again. Death cannot separate us. We really aren't separated now, you know there's such a thin veil between us. I know you can't see me right now, but I am here, near you most of the time. Yes, know that we *will* be together again.

I am very busy now, going to classes, continuing my counseling duties, and the usual day-to-day necessities. Time passes very quickly here, so that it doesn't seem like time, at all. Your deep-seated grief makes it harder now for me to reach you. The more you question and doubt, the more you shut me out. I can only reach you when you are *open and receptive*. The more you trust and believe, the easier it is to bridge the distance between us.

I heard you expressing regrets that you didn't "do more" for me. How on earth do you think you could have done anything more than you did? Please, don't ever think that in some way you "let me down". You didn't, and I am so honored that you loved me, and more than that, that we were friends. And I loved you totally, completely and forever.

I get uneasy over your hopelessness and grief. There's so much work for you to do. Your "silent" death wish is dangerous to the plan. You aren't taking care of yourself, as if you deliberately want to give the body the opportunity to fail. You say you won't commit suicide, but, what you are doing is practically the same thing. I wish I could "pump you up" with some of your old "get up and go" enthusiasm. My mission is to work with you to get information out to the people one earth. Your doubts are a barrier I can't cross. You don't even trust these letters anymore, do you?

I saw you reading the card I gave you on our wedding day. It was me that urged you to read it, so you would remember what I wrote, I said I would love you "forever and forever". That was truth then and it is truth now. It will be truth for as long as we both exist.

Until you get over this "hump" of grief, regrets and doubts, I can't begin the teaching transmissions. What would it take to make you believe in me?

I wasn't "sent" to take care of you, I *found* you because I needed you, your love and your help to make a "clean get away"! I think we both knew the first day we met that there was some kind of connection between us. Neither of us was "ready" for a love such as ours at that time. Too many things had to be completed and learned before we could finally come together.

I know you want to "see" me again tonight, but the grief you are feeling doesn't allow me to come into your vision. I can only project into your thoughts. I'm not sure we can repeat the visual expereince again.

I feel frustrated because I can't seem to help you right now. I ache to comfort you, and I feel your doubts even as you are writing. I keep wanting to yell when you stop, keep writing, don't break the connection!

Won't you meditate more on this? I know your Source will somehow give you what you need to believe that these messages are truly real. Many of my friends here are practically holding their collective breaths to see if you *will* be open to continuing these conversations. They feel the tremendous need for it to happen, just like I do. It's *not just for us*, it is for *all* that are dragged down in sorrow over the loss of a loved one.

James

Marian: *(Note to reader)*   *As I went through all of the classic steps of grieving, the shock, pain, anger, and denial the letters were often confusing. One day I would be excited and looked forward to using them to help others know a little more about the process called death. I would carefully recopy my hastily scribbled notes. The next day I would "hit the skids" and with full denial surging forth I would crumble up the papers and throw them in the trash can. Only to pull them out later, and begin again. Several times I actually felt the soft, gentle vibration that indicated the way was open to write, but would absolutely refuse to be any part of it! The fact that any of this was ever completed is the most amazing fact of all.*

Marian: *Several weeks of peace has passed since last I "wrote" for James. Many guests and Christmas holiday arrangements had kept me very busy. Emotionally I was in a stable place, and I had been able to sleep better. The holidays have always been a joyous time for me, and I was caught up in the excitement of secrets, pretty paper, bright ribbons and our charities, as well as family gatherings.*

Finally, I went to my desk, picked up the pen, and called James. As always, he arrived instantly with the usual aura of soft gentleness. I had no particular question, so asked him if he could give any more information about his new life.

James: I am still preparing for the Hall of Memories, but I'm also involved in other training as well. We have been attending a series of classes concerned with communication between Summerland and the Earth plane. You know, you said many were going to become "incredibly psychic". As the psychic awareness on your plane increases, more and more communications between planes *will* be possible. As earthlings become increasingly aware of the more spiritual planes, ignorance and fear will begin to fade away. It is the hope here that many fine teachers, will commit themselves to "crossing the frontiers of fear", and opening up vast reservoirs of knowledge to flood the human consciousness with Truth. It didn't take long, once I knew it was possible, for me to volunteer to act like a "guide" for you into the Higher realms. Knowing your strong commitment to teach, I knew I could count on you to "pass it on" if I could span the veil and communicate about our world here in Summerland.

By the way, I recently learned Summerland is, also, known as the Third Heaven. Those who arrive here are past the need to re-embody, and their striving is ever upward toward union with God! My soul rejoices in that knowledge, but how I long for you, my darling, to make this journey with me. I don't want to go where you can't find me.

I like my revitalized body very much. I guess I now look the way

I always wanted to look. A few muscles, you know. I never experience tiredness, but I do have daily "sleep" periods that are very refreshing. I've even added a couple of new garments to my wardrobe. In addition to favorite pants and shirts, I now have several long, flowing robe-like garments of a silky-soft material, mostly whites and silvery blue. Clothing never soils here, so we don't need much, just a few for variety. Since there is no "dirty" talk and actions here, there are no "soiled" conditions, either. Everything just stays sparkling clean, better than any washer or cleaner.

We bathe frequently, not so much to cleanse ourselves, but because the waters are electro-magnetically charged, and they stimulate our vibrancy and awareness. A bath here is to increase perceptions and light.

We do eat, but not as often or the heavy foods of the earth plane. My love of fruit has allowed me to partake of many varieties I've never known before. Honey-sweet and juicy, I find the fruits filling and comforting. I don't seem to have any need here for protein or starches. But, I still love my sweets! They are available whenever the urge hits me. You know how I loved chocolate!

The streets *aren't made of gold,* as earth legends would have us believe. They are more like beautiful garden paths. People don't live all "bunched up" in rabbit warrens, but each one finds their own quiet, secluded place of beauty, and creates the home of their dreams. I love my country cottage and all of the beauty around it.

I have two "pets" now. A little white dove often sits on my shoulder, softly cooing, when I'm sitting in my garden. She seems absolutely without fear, but I sit very still so I won't frighten her away. I don't know what she eats, since we don't seem to have any insects or bugs here. I guess she must eat seeds and fruits, also. This morning I held out my hand, and she sat on my finger for the longest time. Tears came, because it felt so gentle and loving.

I found a black and white kitten on the path awhile ago. He reminds me of Blackjack*, so that's what I call him. He seems to love to hide under the bushes and jump out at me. He sleeps on the foot of my sleeping lounge, and is a lot of company. This morning I was almost sure he said, "Good morning, James", but maybe it was just my imagination.

James

* Blackjack is the house cat James left behind when he made his transition.

Marian: *A few days passed, filled with day to day duties. I prayed James would "do well" in the Hall of Memories and asked God to watch over him. On this particular day I had no questions. I was simply open and receptive, ready to write. In my mind I still wondered about the Hall of Memories, and had the impression it was over.*

My personal grief seemed to be easing a bit. I was getting the sense I wanted to "get back to work" in counseling, catching up on paperwork and writing. I felt angelic comfort close to me, and each time I prayed or meditated I kept hearing the small voice within saying in my mind, "The worst is over. You are not alone. God loves you and so do we." I felt like my personal angels were comforting and encouraging me to go forward.

James: Well, here I am once more, definitely a bit chastened. You have no idea how happy I am that the Hall of Memories ordeal is over! Yes, it was an ordeal, for I had to see myself as I *really* was, not how I *thought* I was. Definitely some attitudes I needed to correct.

When I emerged I was literally a "basket case", stumbling out into the comforting arms of the Lady. I ached for all the mistakes I had made, and the hundreds of opportunities I had missed to comfort, love and aid others. The smugness of my former judgments and opinions as well as the arrogance of my ego cut me to the depths of my being. If we could only know the harm we're doing when we speak so critically and sharply! How much differently we would live our lives. Oh, that we could do it all over, in the light of Love!

I was taken immediately to the chapel at the restoration clinic. I was left alone in a quiet sanctuary setting, weeping, thinking, and regretting.

After a while I was summoned to meet Radha, and begin dialogue about my feelings. She was deeply compassionate, but gave "very little quarter" in forcing me to face what I had just seen and relived. As I talked to her, I began to regain control of myself, and I asked what I could do to make it up.

She pulled me into her arms, like I was a small boy, and held me close for the longest time. Then quietly she said:

Dear One, you have seen the error of anger, fear and ego. You have felt the pain they cause. You have seen the shallowness of your motives. And you, also, saw, as your life progressed, how you had made big changes in all of these areas. If you hadn't you wouldn't be here now.

Remember this, James, it was all for growth and learning...for everyone involved in each situation. You have seen pain that you never meant to inflict. You have seen what the lack of tenderness did to everyone around you. You have viewed what the lack of tenderness toward you did to your whole life. You are feeling sorrow and regrets, and long for forgiveness. That you already have. Now your great work begins.

First, go and tell our dear Marian so that she may write, teach and help others to avoid these pitfalls, while they still can.

*Then return here to consult with your counselor, and together you will evaluate the life just passed to see what was gained from it. Fortunately for you, the Law of Forgiveness was invoked and granted in the last several years, so Grace has removed you from Karmic return. Remember, lessons are **always** waiting to be learned, no matter what plane the soul is on.*

Dear One, earth lifetimes are classrooms used to hone the soul into the sharp clarity necessary for union with God. To this purpose our Beloved Jesus went to Earth, in order to show the way. Now, as you move into total understanding and love, you, also, will become a Way-Shower, as will so many, many others.

Your cosmic union with Marian was to complete a circuitry through which greater Truth might be released to those still bound in flesh and blood. The love you two share, and both of your unique psychic giftings has provided us with a long awaited Open Line between heaven and earth.

Now, beloved one, dry your tears and return to the council room where your advisors await you. They will give you a soothing potion and return you to your cottage where you will rest. During the rest period there will be electro-magnetic currents directed into your mind and heart. These currents will bring great comfort, and when you awaken you will once more be filled with joyous love and peace. The recently viewed experiences will become a guide line that will greatly help many who are still enslaved. Your beloved Marian will hold the Light for you as you rest. When you commence communications again, you will move from incidental reportings to much Higher Truths from the Fifth Dimension.

As she released me, and touched my heart center with her fingers, I felt a sense of relief flood my whole being.

I must go now, but I will write again as soon as I have done as she instructed. Bless you for standing guard during this ordeal. For myself, I'm so grateful it's finally over!

James

Marian: *Today was Bruce's birthday, and I was once more trying to understand the grief process. Feeling on the edge of sadness, I felt the need to make contact with James. As always I immediately felt the soft, gentle essence of his presence and immediately picked up the pen. Hearing his voice in my mind, I asked him, if he feels loneliness or grief, or any other sense of loss and separation there in Summerland? How does the passing of time enter the picture?*

James: You know, I've been mentioning the "no time" phenomena here. I don't even begin to understand it, but one thing I can tell you, I really like it!

No one here has any sense of separation or longing or loneliness. Since everything is right *now*, we have no concept of time passing. It seems like I've always been here. Yet it also seems like I just this moment arrived. But "arrived" isn't a very good way to describe it, either, because I don't have any sense of *going any where*. I'm not sure how to put into words this miraculous, gloriously happy beingness I now experience.

How on earth... or should I say heaven, can I feel loss when I've never *left* you or my dear friends and family? I touch your hand, your head, your shoulder many times just to reassure you that I am always "with" you. True, you usually aren't even aware of my presence. Sometimes I see the shadow of grief cross your face for a moment as you fleetingly think of me, then it is gone and you go on with the tasks at hand. In that moment, I know your soul has felt my touch. I want to shout "Yes, I am here! I've not left you! Don't be sad! Can't you see how alive I am?"

Here in this blessed beautiful place grief has no hold on us. We live a life of joy, love and serenity, bound not by memories of what we've "lost", but the utter happiness of being *alive*! You sang "Fully alive in the Spirit" at Sunday services. Virginia, dear Virginia, waved her tambourine and everyone was smiling and moving with the rhythm of the music. In that moment you got a tiny taste of being fully alive in the Spirit! True, we don't beat the tambourine, clap our hands, and dance to the music, we just "be" in that joyful, peaceful symphony of Life.

How can I feel loss when actually I only lost the pain, fear, and sorrows? In return I found peace and life so exquisitely beautiful it defies mere words. In reality, beloved, I haven't lost you, I've found you at last! For now, I touch your soul, and know who you *really* are, so far beyond my ability to "see" you in our brief earthly marriage.

I don't pretend to have the answers about this reality I'm now experiencing. As I've heard you say so many times, " I don't even have the questions". I'm accepting the *timelessness*, living in it and I've about stopped trying to figure it out. It just is! I think I now know what you tried to explain to me about "drifting upon the currents of Life, in the great Sea of Love and Mercy". You said it was the Eternal Spirit, God, and it was Life Everlasting. At the time my heart was touched by the poetry of your words, but I truly didn't comprehend the meaning. Now...now I am living in your magical sea (or world) of love and mercy! You see, there really is such a place!

I've asked Radha if this is heaven. She just smiles and softly replies *"Is heaven not in your own consciousness: a sweet surrender to the true Spirit of the Creator? Heaven, such a lovely word, is just an **earthly** description of spiritual oneness, where only peace, harmony, beauty and Life can be experienced. Heaven is the Divine Creation of the wandering ones returning to their Source. One day, all men and women will know this and darkness will no longer reign upon the plane of of form and matter".* When she speaks so gently and lovingly, again I feel like a small boy, learning at his mother's knee.

As for grief, it just isn't possible here. Since I have lost nothing and gained everything, ancient fears and grief are only words with absolutely no meaning in my life. Like a line from a frontier novel. "Check Your Weapons at the Door", my weapons of grief, fear and anger were left behind at the moment of my liberation! I did not bring them with me! I hope this answers your questions, my love. Remember, we take the Love with us!

James

Marian: *After spending the next five months moving to the mountains of North Carolina and establishing Terra Nova Center, I finally found time to get back to the writings. Overwhelmed by the material, I was tempted to discard it all and chalk it up to just another life experience. Suddenly I heard James's voice in my mind saying "Don't throw it all away! I don't know the details, but Radha does. Please, ask her what to do".*

As if on cue, I heard Radha say "What is it you wish to know, dear one"? I responded by asking, "Radha, what am I suppose to do with all of this information? Why was it given like this? Why me"?

Radha: Beloved one, don't you remember so many years ago, in your beginning womanhood time, when you were told "No grave would ever contain you"? That you would teach this to thousands of others? That time has come and the teaching has already begun. All over your planet, people are questioning, wondering, and hoping that death is not the end, but, perhaps a beginning of something far greater.

Your beloved Grandmother was once your teacher in the long ago Temple of Ashelon, in a place those on earth called Atlantis. She was preparing you then for the very work that you are embarked upon now. *She* couldn't teach these things, for the people were still locked in fear of death, and the darkness of their own mortality. *She was preparing you to remember, and to teach.*   Only through personal experiences that you *knew* were so, could you share with any kind of authority and believability. For this you have been trained and prepared through many, many birth and death experiences. The people of your planet are awakening, remembering and learning. They are starved for more knowledge that will help to set them free from the ancient taboos and fears. They are ready! Your time to teach is *now!*

James, so much a part of yourself and also, once a priest of Ashelon, was brought to you to play an important role in this process. So psychically connected through your deep love for one another, he is an excellent sender, you the receiver. Together you build a Bridge of Consciousness (love) between the worlds. The Bridge is wide and sound. Tens of thousands will recognize the truth of this bridge, and in the doing their terrible fears of the unknown will begin to divide and fall away.

You and James are keyed to the same soul pattern, and long ago, you both agreed to come together, only to be torn apart, so that the Bridge of Awareness could be built. You were both well prepared for the pain and grief that would be necessary in order to rent the veil of darkness, (or should I say ignorance), that divides the planes of Life. Only through the suffering could the victory be won. Much as childbearing labor is painful, but the birth of the child is joyous, so it is with life and the liberation you so erroneously call death. For, beloved one, there is only life dancing outwardly, then back to the Source, then once again moving back into physical expression. No beginning. No ending. Ever! Only life, learning, growing, changing until, at last, the soul *knows* it is immortal and Everlasting!

So many ages humanity has lived in terror of being "lost" in death. Most religions have perpetuated the lies about life and death! Now a new day of understanding is dawning upon your beautiful planet. The tattered garments of false beliefs and terror are being stripped away. The people, the dear, dear, blessed people, are awakening from their long sleep! Now those teachers prepared so long ago can freely write and teach of Life continuing onward and upward into immortality! In time the dread of death will disappear from your precious planet. Then death will no longer be the enemy, but instead the welcoming Angel of Liberation into grander and more wondrous knowingness for every single soul.

Go now and teach all who will listen that they can never die, for *they* are the Immortals! Write these things, and share the love, for hundreds of thousands long for the blessed insights you now have to share. As you share with others, your own faith will also expand.

Help each one to know that they may call upon their angels at all times to help them through the fears, rage and grief...that they have only to ask. Every word that you write will help dissolve the terrible wall of fear that humanity has built around the glorious homecoming experience they call death. Yes, dear one, tell them they are *all* Immortals.

Radha

Marian: *Radha, what, in your opinion, is the most important lesson to be learned from this process called death? I've often referred to our world as a "Great university of Life" and as a Life University student, I don't want to "miss a single trick". I realize many are watching to see how I handle these experiences. I just want to be sure I "see" it clearly, and speak Truth to those who want to know. Would you please, dear teacher, share whatever you will to help not only me, but others who face the same questions and issues?*

Radha: Beloved one, I smile as your write, for no matter how hurting and painful your life is, you are always the teacher, aren't you? We who guide and watch are pleased.

O, my dear, if only souls could learn to be tender and gentle with one another and themselves! If only they could trust that the Blessed Creator *does not destroy, but constantly creates good.* If only they could feel great joy when a soul leaves the earthly body and returns to the blessed peace of the Higher Realms!

What terrible traps, created out of fear and disbelief, bind humanity! The greatest lesson of all is to learn, and understand about cycles of Life, continuity, eternal Beingness. What you call death is only another doorway, into yet another phase of Life! Liberation from the shell of form and matter is a tremendous gift of love from the Creator! With this gift sorrow, pain, despair, hopelessness, anger, fear and degeneration are removed, and instantly the soul is freed to experience other levels of Life. Life, filled with beauty , peace, and joy!

When James suggested you think of him now as "working out of town", he was imparting a far greater truth than even he realized! On earth loved ones often reside thousands of miles apart from one another and there is no grief, for each one knows the other is alive, that only miles separate. O, that earthlings could begin to comprehend that their loved ones have only stepped through the very thin veil of ethers, and that they live on, just a heart beat away! Here beyond the veil of invisibility that separates the planes of life, the departed ones still dance, sing, write, learn, hope, and serve! Yes, and even play, but without competition, just for the sheer joy of it.

What is the greatest lesson? Relish life and be happy for the new life opportunities of the departed ones. Celebrate their wonderful new opportunity to rest and learn. Every soul returns again and again to their *real home*! Earth is a lovely place to go to school, but dear one, how wonderful when the class is over, and the student returns home to the welcoming love of the Father!

There is an old gospel hymn on earth called "I will take my vacation in Heaven". Each soul leaving the bondage of flesh, finds themselves in such a situation. Home once more with loved ones who have gone on before, in gentle, peaceful, pain free, surroundings. No wonder it seems like a long awaited "vacation in heaven"!

The most important lesson to be learned by the death of a loved one? They did not, *could not,* die! They live, healed and free, in their true home! Only a thin veil of invisibility separates you. Their love is greater than ever for those left behind. Beyond that veil pain and anger drops away like ragged garments, a new garment of joy and understanding now clothe their beautiful new bodies! Not ghostly forms! Feeling, solid bodies, without blemish, unseen only because they vibrate on a higher frequency than your human eyes can see. Listen with your heart, open, receptive, willing to accept their new place in the Circle of Life.

Know this truth! Tell others! One day this fearful specter of ignorance will dissolve and all of humanity will celebrate the freedom of their own divine Eternalness.

Radha

Marian: *Over two years passed before I again felt the urge to pick up the pen, and attempt to make another contact with James. Busy at the new Terra Nova Center in the Blue Ridge Mountains of North Carolina, I was totally absorbed in the day-to-day items of business. My grief was slowly healing and I no longer was in the deeply wounded space I had been in during the earlier communications. Thoughts about the book were simply "put on the back burner", **hopefully** to be forgotten by everyone.*

*From time to time I "saw" James in dreams, and would wake up, aware we had actually been together in the spiritual world. It always felt so good. For several months prior to receiving the following message I, again, felt "pressured" to write. Friends would call me on the phone, and ask how the book was coming along. I felt guilty because I was so evasive, I did **not** want to write a book! **Especially this book**! Time after time I would feel a presence, and would automatically reach for the pen, only to drop it and emphatically state **"O, no you don't! You're not going to get me back into that silly drama again! I've just got my life back. I'm not going to have the whole world thinking I'm crazy! No sir, I'm not going to write anymore"**!*

But, in February 1995 the old familiar patterns of "contact" assaulted my senses again. First the dreams. James and Radha smiling at me and saying "It's time, you know". Falling books, the TV coming on by itself, even the whiff of James' favorite cologne! (O, no, here we go again!) I would sit down to write to a friend, and my thoughts would stray from the task at hand, to well, maybe I'll just try one more time. I can always throw it away. No one will be the wiser. For days my dialogue with myself continued. I kept feeling the presence of a loving being. James? Radha? But, God, all I want is a normal life! But, the urges to write got stronger and stronger.

Finally in late February I sat at my desk with pen in hand, and wrote: *"OK! I'm here, just like you wanted. I'm going to do this just one more time, and then I'm through! Do you understand that? You say I've got free will. Well, dear ones, my free will is that I be a simple normal person and normal people don't go around writing and receiving letters from heaven! Have you got that? Have I made myself clear? So, what do you want from me now"?*

James: (Laughingly) My, you are temperamental! I fully understand where you are coming from but, beloved one, we haven't finished what we agreed to do. There is so much yet to be given to help people move upward into higher consciousness. *Please*, reconsider finishing the book. *What do you have to lose?* You are already a very loved and highly respected teacher. Those who are ready will read, and know our worlds are truly one. Those who still sleep in their egos, will toss it aside with scorn just as they have rejected *all* new ideas down through the ages. So, what is the difference? Hasn't it always been that way on earth?

Marian: *I guess that's true. Forgive me for "bailing out" on the job. I know we agreed to do this but I wish it wasn't such a scary thing for me. And, I do feel your wonderful love! I guess I'll just have "another go at it". So, what's on the burner for today?*

James: Today we were shown something that truly excited me, and I am anxious to share it with you for I know you will pass it on. In fact, I considered it to be like a great miracle! From far out in space, beyond the sun we were shown enormous iridescent golden white and translucent rays of energy steaming toward the earth. Someone said it came from Jupiter, but I just thought of it as from the heart of the Creator! *It was falling all over the earth.* Gentle, soft, incredibly beautiful mist enfolding every atom of space on earth! The Lady, in answer to my unspoken question, said it was a direct response to the people's prayers. The beautiful spiritual energy beaming forth like Cosmic rays were to *soften, and heal hardened hearts and to open up closed, narrow minds on earth!*

We were then told that only by bombarding the earth with such a loving healing vibration could old patterns, destructive thinking, cruelty and selfishness be changed to bring about the great healing necessary for the freedom of the earth. As the constant patterns of destruction give way to new patterns of joy and unselfishness, the Light will definitely increase

We had so many questions about the Light it was hard to put them all in order. I knew you would be excited about this phenomena as well, so I'm going to try to answer a few of the questions I imagine *you* might have.

Q.   *Why? Why is this happening now?*
A.   Because it is time, and the people have longed, hoped and prayed for it.

Q.   *Will it stop?*
A.   Only if the people refuse to accept the new pattern of change.

Q.   *How will the Spiritual Guardians know the people desire these changes?*
A.   The people will keep asking. Only through their petitions can Cosmic help be given. Free will you know.

Q.   *How long will the radiation take place?*
A.   As long as it takes whether it be ten earth years or a hundred.

Q.   *How will the people feel while the softening process is taking place?*
A.   Tremendous strain will be experienced on every level. Physically, bodies will feel tired as hidden aches and pains are rooted out. Sleep will often be sporadic and fitful as the new energy "stretches" and rebuilds the old cellular patterns. Mentally and emotionally, individuals will experience anxieties and fears, as the old familiar patterns are dredged up from the

memory banks, to be transmuted into the higher frequency. As you have so often said, most will go "kicking and screaming" into higher consciousness. Spiritually, there will be literally millions awakening to some knowledge of God and the need to be more loving and caring of one another.

Q. *Will the radiation's stop? Is there a specific time when it is strongest, like say on the full moon?*
A. The spirals of light are released every 27 - 29 of your earth days starting strongly for a few days, and then ebbing in order to give the people a chance to adapt to it. If the moon has anything to do with it, I was not made aware of it. No, it won't stop. It will last as long as it takes to transform the earth into a true Heavenly Body. It is projected here that this could be accomplished within three generations.

Q. *How about the hard core haters, manipulators, and controllers? What if they refuse to change?*
A. They will simply die, and re-embody on another lower energy planet, until they are ready to surrender to Love.

Q. *How does this new energy affect the rest of us?*
A. As the new love vibration penetrates the hearts and souls of those seeking change, attitudes, old conflicts, and behavior will give way to more loving and harmonious interaction between all.

Q. *What then?*
A. Heaven on earth will begin, or as you call it, ascension! It truly will be the full expression of "as above, so below".

Q. *Will the dark ones then return?*
A. No. Spirit is like water, it seeks it's own level. Love and peace can only attract the same as its self. Darkness can only draw close to its own unique pattern. Thus as it is said on earth, "never the 'twain shall meet".

Q. *Is it working?*

A. Far more than you can imagine!

Q. *How do the guides feel about the massive changes? Do they ever despair because we seem to be so slow in our awakening?*
A. Far from it! The element of excitement over this transformational process is like a contagion! We all are radiantly joyous as we watch the changes taking place. Since we do not know time, it seems to be happening right NOW, and that is wondrous to behold. Hopes are very high over here! It's like watching a beautiful jewel beginning to form! Very exciting!

Q. *What should I do?*
A. Exactly what you are doing right now. Pray. Love. Forgive. Teach. And always, hold the Grand Vision in your consciousness. Speak the words of transformation in your heart, in your prayers, and in your day-to-day contact with others. Even as you experience the great strains on the emotions, and in the body, never give up hope and never stop praying!

Q. *Should this information be made public?*
A. Absolutely! Many, many inspired teachers on earth are receiving the same message. Shout it from the mountain tops! Those who can hear will, and those who refuse won't! Get the message out! Planet Earth is making its long awaited ascension!

Marian: *That is heart warming news, and I can feel your excitement! Yes, I will get this message out, I promise. By the way, **If**, now mind you, I said **if**, I **do** finish the book can you promise me I won't be held up to ridicule? Maybe people won't want it, anyway, will they?*

James: O, the people want the "good news"... they are desperate to know what lies beyond the veil. No I can't make promises about what happens afterwards. You are very, very protected and deeply loved, in both worlds. Just trust God's perfect will and love to care for you all of the days of your life. Please, don't be afraid. All is well. This is a very good thing that you do, my love! Please know many people want and need a book like this.

James

Marian: *I had a very vivid dream last night. I saw James standing at a cross roads, looking somewhat confused about which direction he should go. Upon awakening, I was troubled, but couldn't quite put my finger on what was wrong. Finally, I sat down, pen in hand, and after prayer, I silently called to him with my mind. Immediately he seemed to be there. I told him of the dream, and how uneasy it was making me feel.*

James: It is strange that you are having these feelings because what seems like only a moment ago, I met with our dear Radha. She told me the "doorway" that we have opened between the worlds would soon need to close. She said you needed to emotionally break away from me in order to facilitate a complete healing for yourself. And I have a lovely opportunity to enter the Golden Center of Wisdom for my own growth. If I choose the Wisdom Center, I will not be communicating with you in the same manner or as freely as we have in the past.

Since I know "no time" it will be a simple matter for me. My concern, if I dare use such a term, is that you will once more feel abandoned. That is the very last thing I want for you. Radha explained that the Doorway of Communication had been arranged by *special dispensation* because the information was to be one more tool to break the fear of death cycle on earth. She explained that it was now time to close the door, so that each of us can continue to experience our own worlds to the fullest. I'm not sure I fully understand "special dispensation" but I believe it means we've had a great deal of spiritual help all along the way with these messages.

She assured me that even though I would communicate infrequently from here on out, our soul fusion will keep us connected on the deeper spiritual level. She said you would, as the withdrawal begins, think less about me, and that the deep-seated grief would slowly fade away. She, also, said she would continue as a mentor for you, and she would be there to guide you along on your spiritual quest, as well as seeing the book through to completion. Yes, she said you *would* finish the book.

I have longed for wisdom and understanding for so very long. My soul thrills at the prospect of entering the hallowed halls of the Center of Wisdom.

It is such a glorious place, high on a hill, much removed from where I am now. The buildings look like sparkling alabaster, and at sundown a golden glow radiates out in all directions. The center is walled, but the gates are always open. I'm told only if one has a pass or permission can they enter the open gates. We often hear beautiful music and the sound of temple bells ringing down the mountain side. My soul thrills to know I've earned the right to study there. It is considered a great privilege to, as we put it, "go up the mountain". The prospect of going there nearly takes my breath away. Radha assures me she will keep an eye on you and will remain as a liaison between us. She said occasionally I will be able to reach your thoughts, but mostly my new studies will keep me occupied. As I said before, I won't be aware of time's passage, but you will. Just remember, we are one, and please, share these messages with as many people as possible. I am always only a heartbeat away. And, please, finish the book quickly. *Now* is the hour!

Marian: *James, before you leave could I ask a couple of questions? First, going to the Golden Temple, does that mean you no longer will work in the Grey Zone? Secondly, will you actually leave your cottage and live behind the walls at the center?*

James: Good questions, but I'm not sure I have the answers. There is a mysterious aura around the Temple, and us "commoners" have little contact with the students there. Everyone here looks up to the center, like it was a Holy Shrine, and most of us hope someday to be there. What I have noticed is once someone leaves our community to go there, we don't see them again. Like everything else in this world, it seems like it may be a portal, or doorway, to yet a Higher Plane.

As for the teaching in the Grey Zone, I at this point haven't the faintest idea what happens now. Since everything is in perfect balance and order here at all times, I know there can't be such a thing as unfinished business. Therefore whether I return to do the work, or someone else does it, it *will* be done. When I move to the temple my lovely cottage will dissolve back into the ethers. At least this is what I've been told. It was manifested out of the etheric substance, and when no longer needed it simply dissapears. No, empty abandoned houses here!

Marian: *What about your pets? Do they go with you?*

James: I just don't know. In fact I've been so excited I've not even considered details. I can't imagine Blackjack not following me there. He goes every where I go, including into my sessions with Radha. I've become so used to him being with me, that he's like an "extra appendage". Speaking of pets, most everyone here seems to have a special companion, usually a beloved pet that had passed over while the individual was still on earth.

The bond of love between a person and an animal does not break at death. So, when both meet in the spirit world, the love continues on just as before. Animals here are never noisy, rowdy, messy or pests. I've only seen cats and dogs and an occasional bird as personal companions, so far. I guess I'll just "wait and see" whether Blackjack goes "up the mountain" with me.

Does that answer your questions?

Marian: *Yes, I think so. Thank you my love.*

Marian: *Several hours after the last message from James, my mind was still jumbled up with questions. Just before bedtime I again sat down, pen in hand and quietly called to him. Instantly it felt like he was right beside me, and as always, my hand again started writing.*

James: (Laughingly) What took you so long? I knew you weren't satisfied with the answers I gave you earlier, so I've been expecting to hear from you again.

Marian: *I want to talk more about animals. So many people want to know what happens when a beloved pet dies. Would you tell me a little bit more about this please?*

James: Animals have a very, very tender and special place in the lives of humans. I speak particularly of dogs and cats. Every single part of life has a purpose, including our pets. Learning to love and care for an animal is an important step toward compassion, tenderness and selflessness. The humans that are cruel to animals or neglectful to their pets have closed hearts and they are not able to see the divine opportunity Life places before them through the animal kingdom.

Not all teachers come to us as humans, or as angels. Animals are teachers, also. When a human loses a beloved pet, that golden chord of love does not break. As long as the love is experienced, the chord remains, connecting one with the other in spite of the animal having left the body. Often the pet will stay close to the human master, acting like a protector and spiritual guide. When the human master dies, the relationship is quickly renewed in the spiritual world. As long as the love and appreciation is present, master and pet are companions to one another. The key to the relationship is love.

Marian: *How about fleas and wastes? How are they dealt with? When an animal gets old, sickly and in constant pain, what then? What if* the pet's master feels the need to have the animal put to sleep in order to relieve it's suffering, then what happens?

James: Absolutely nothing! *When the action is an act of mercy* the love chord remains intact and unbroken. The human masters must make these decisions from time to time in order to set their beloved companions free. If it is done in compassion and love, the animal knows this and is very grateful to be free of the suffering. The love relationship continues unbroken.

As I have mentioned before this is a balanced and very efficient world. Nothing that does not fit the balance of beauty and purity can exist here. Fleas and wastes are not necessary, nor are they part of the balance. This is a spotless world. Wastes simply don't exist, and pests such as fleas have no function here. Imagine, the immaculately groomed, well mannered pet who can "talk" to you! Sounds like heaven, doesn't it? What, no more questions?

Marian: *Well, just one. I've noticed I sometimes ask questions and you say you don't know. I thought when we returned to the heavenly worlds we knew everything, we didn't remember or know while on earth. Would you comment, please?*

James: That is another fallacy humankind has about the spiritual realms, or heaven, as they call it. We do not suddenly become all-seeing and all-knowing just because we have left the body behind. The Universal mind, like a vast wisdom pool, is available to all who seek, and no matter how high one might evolve, there is always more to be experienced and learned. Truly a living, moving expanding Intelligence that we may seek to understand *in part*, but I think it would not be possible to "know" it all, simply because it is endless. A vast pulsing Isness, far beyond our abilities to comprehend in it's entirety.

When we arrive here, our intelligence factor is intact *as it was* when we dropped the body. Being "dead" doesn't instantly bring wisdom! We constantly seek, ask, and learn. Our ability to comprehend truths is quite acute. Learning is quicker, and far easier than when we were contained in a physical form. The only thing different here is a great *desire* to know truth! So we constantly learn, comprehend and understand bit by bit the makeup of this thing called life. Just like on earth, we must *want* to know about something before it is revealed to us.

Marian: *Then why hasn't mankind become more aware than it is? Why is there so much ignorance and fear?*

James: Closed minds and fear-filled egos don't miraculously "open" upon return to the spirit world. Only when the soul evolves to a state of awareness of it's *spiritual* identity can progress be made. The closed minded ones keep embodying and dying, over and over until, on earth they finally "wake up" and *want* to learn about love and brotherhood. Then the real progression begins on the homeward journey!

James

The Closing of the Door

Radha: *Greeting, Beloved Child of Light! I come forth as Radha to speak once more with you. It is I who suggested (or should I say commanded) that you must emotionally "let James go". You heard our message clearly but did not understand why. This moment in your time I will try to fill in "the missing pieces".*

First, try to understand that the essence that was James and the essence that is Marian are joined in the mystical wedding of soul that melds you, in spirit, as one. That means that you will never "lose" one another. However...

As long as one of you is on the earth plane and one is in spirit, you both will continue to grow. Even though James dwells in essence with you, he too, must continue to go forward. He has a wonderful opportunity to learn much at this time, but it will mean he will not be writing and speaking with you as frequently. I, Radha, who calls you Daughter of Light and child of my heart, will continue to speak through you, if you will permit this. Much teaching will come now through your spoken messages in groups.

James, so tender in his love for you is reluctant to go on, leaving you in your aloneness. Only you can set him free. As you do this, my love, you will experience a great freedom, and accelerated teaching abilities. Our only concern at this point, is that you, once more, may feel abandoned and rejected. Nothing could be farther from the truth!

As dear James grows and expands, you, too, will experience his increased Light, for it is in the very heart of both of you. As we, you and I, continue the work toward the books, I will keep you apprised of his journey. In this process, however, you won't "see" him as you have in the past. Your memories will dim, and he will become a pleasant memory for you. Then, just as with Bruce, you will begin to heal on all levels.

Do you understand what we ask of you? Ponder on these things,

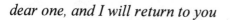

dear one, and I will return to you

In Everlasting Light, I Am
Radha

Marian: *James, as I have been instructed, I am now willing to disengage emotionally from you in order to get on with my life. You will forever be in the very heart of me. Radha reports our work accelerates, but will change in form from here on out. I think she will give most of the future teaching dictations, but I'm not sure. I promise I will seriously attempt to finish the book and give it to the world.*

James: My beloved, this is a joyous moment, even though it may have the appearance of being sad. I have heard your directive for me to realize we both must continue our growth, and that you now release me to other things. Obedient to the end, aren't you?

Dear Radha will continue the transmissions and I will only visit you from time to time in dreamtime. My essence and my love will never leave you. Even though you might not hear my voice or see my form, it doesn't mean we're "lost" to one another. I go now up the sacred mountain where I will be trained for greater service to the Radiant Spirit called God. As I learn, so you will also rapidly increase in your understanding. At first you may experience a sense of loss, but I have not "bailed out" on you! (Radha reports you might even see me from time to time).

Be at peace, my beloved, our souls truly dance as one. My heart sings with the knowledge that our work together will be given to those who are ready. Thank you, Thank you, Thank you!

Always
James

Epilogue

Marian: *Radha, James and I have both wondered what kind of Karma led us into such a wonderful happiness, only to have it torn away so abruptly. Is it possible for you to shed some light on the situation?*

Radha: I would at this time share with you a past life experience in order for both you and James to learn and grow. You must remember, nothing can be given or revealed until the law has been fulfilled. And that law is "Ask and it shall be given". You have asked, and now I will tell you all. Let us call this story *"Sailing into the wind"*.

Sailing Into The Wind
A Love Story

When Life changes abruptly on you, and crisis comes uninvited into your lives, you are forced to make changes. Often drastic measures are called for, and you experience panic and fear. You have two choices. You can run away and "stuff it" or you can "set sail straight into the wind" and face the challenge head on.

If you run away or duck the change, be assured you will get the opportunity to meet it again in another time and another place. The wise one knows this, and chooses to "take the wheel" of their "ship of life", and with courage, dare to sail straight into the stormy seas of change.

I would share with you the love story of someone who chose *not* to face life's ordeals with strength and courage, and how it has affected both parties in this present lifetime.

In a small village in Russia in the early seventeen hundreds there lived a very sensitive and psychic young girl called Marieshka. She "knew" things and had the gift of Far Vision. Raped by soldiers at age fourteen, she bore a child out of wedlock, and was outcast from her village. She lived alone in the forest, shunned and lonely. However, on the sly, villagers would still seek her out to see what she saw with her far vision, and for her healing potions.

When Marieshka was twenty years old, there came to the village a tall handsome stranger. He was a writer from England, gathering the myths and folklore of Europe to put in his newest book. The villagers told him the best storyteller was the woman, Marieshka, and directed him to her cottage. Living alone with only her small son to provide her with love and comfort, she welcomed her unusual visitor.

The writer Chauncey met Marieshka and it was love at first sight for both of them. Deep within the soul of each was recognition and re-membrance of a deep soulmate belonging. It was not long before they married and started a life together in the small forest cottage. Soon a daughter was born and the little family was joyous and complete.

But, homesick for his beloved England, Chauncey began to feel the painful grip of depression take hold of his spirit. He wanted to go home and publish his stories. Often he would beg Marieshka to go with him.

Marieshka was afraid because of her strange dialect and gypsy ori-gin, that people in London would make fun of her. She begged her beloved Chauncey to stay where she felt safe, in her own home. So for the next three years Chauncey stayed on at the cottage teaching his wife and chil-dren to speak English. But, the longing for his own home across the sea persisted. Then one day, Marieshka, knowing how sad he was, agreed to leave Russia and go with him to England.

In London she became a sensation! With her exotic looks and her Far Vision even those who walked with kings and queens sought her out. The people loved her and wanted her to stay.

But Marieshka longed for her village and her forest home and a deep seated sorrow began to take its toll on her body. She became weaker and weaker. Chauncey finally realized she would surely die if she did not return to her homeland. So he took her back to Russia.

But Chauncey was ill, though he said not a word about it to anyone, not even to Marieshka. His cough worsened and he began to spit up blood. Not wanting to worry his beloved wife he said little, telling her he had a cold. One day he simply disappeared telling no one where he was going or why. He returned to England, and quickly died, alone and without his supportive family around him.

Marieshka was devastated after he left. She tried to figure out what on earth she had done to drive him away. In sorrow she, too, began to weaken, and it was not long before she joined him in death.

But the die was cast! Because Chauncey chose to *run away* instead of *facing* his dilemma, it was set in Fate's timeless motion that this test would have to be met again, in another lifetime. Things had been left unfinished and he had denied her a most important life opportunity. He denied her the privilege of taking care of him "in sickness as in health". He took away the opportunity for both to "set sail straight into the wind" All of the lessons to be learned by facing terminal illness and the caretaking of someone facing such a situation were lost, or at least unfinished.

You were Marieshka and your beloved James, was Chauncey. Once more, in this lifetime, you met; Once more you recognized each other and quickly fell in love. But James, as was Chauncey, was seriously ill. Beneath the double pneumonia that he *thought* he had, a deadly cancer was destroying his lungs. *But this time he did not run away.* He dared to courageously set sail straight into the wind and he allowed you the great privilege of taking care of him, as well as the opportunity to walk him through the dying process. Together you faced termination of his physical body in order for both of you to understand there is no death, only change! The letters James has sent from Summerland go far toward proving this to be true.

Radha

104

Marian: *Thank you dear Radha for that lovely story. In my heart I know it is true. For over a year I've had such a deep sense that we have been "re-doing" something that perhaps we didn't complete in another time and another place. Your lovely story feels "true" to me, and I'm so very happy you shared it with me.*

Radha: Every soul on earth could get their own "personal story" if their faith was strong enough, and they *asked, believing* there would be an answer. We, over here, rejoice when someone still embodied believes strongly enough in our reality to ask. So, I, also, say thank-you.

Radha

A Message From Marian

Many of you, in the next few years, are going to be facing similar situations. Some of you will be privileged to know in advance that a loved one has but a short time left in this big university called planet earth. You may do one of two things. You may go into denial and deep depression and in doing so you will miss a fabulous experience. Or you may sail right into the wind and keep your ship of life afloat and experience one of the most transcendent things that can happen to we who are Spirit, merely encased in these mortal forms!

The changes that are around us are enormous. The fall of the Soviet Union as it has been known and the failure of communism is but a symptom of the things around us that are falling into debris to be cleared away. There isn't a single one of us that isn't going to face a challenge of one kind or another, the approaching transition of a loved one, the loss of a job, troubles in relationships, or perhaps changes in your own physical body. If you allow yourself the strength and the knowledge that you are Spirit and dare to sail into the winds of change, you will arrive on the other side so powerful and so transcendent that you will never again have to repeat the experience.

If you run away and try to hide from these things and do not face them square on, it will come to pass that it will return to you to be lived out in yet another lifetime just as it did for Chauncey and Marieshka, for whom the final chapter had to be rewritten so that both could learn and grow.

We are moving out of the third dimensional world. Very few of us have our feet totally anchored in the third dimension anymore. Most of the time we don't know where we are, where we've been or where we are going. We're living in "weird"! James used to say. This time he dared to stay instead of runing away, staying until the final moment. I had the great privilege to be able to experience this with him. We don't have to do that again. It is finished.

These are the things that are happening to us now. We are changing on the cellular level. Some will drop the physical body, some will make changes in where we work and who we work with. We are all making changes, *we have to change.* But we also, have to have courage and strength. We have to have the backbone that comes from the *knowing of who and what we are*! When we finally realize that we are Spirit, then we absolutely *cannot* be conquered by any physical world condition!

The cold stones put over a grave to memorialize or remember a loved one are instead a constant reminder of *death* not of *life.* We are Spirit and we need to remember that we are Spirit. Jesus Christ taught when he was dying, *"I am not of the earth, I am Spirit".* He knew it and He believed it, and so He set His ship full sail into the winds to whatever lay just beyond the horizon.

The reason that I share this is that each of us comes to those moments when it seems easier to say "I'll just keep this from my husband" or "I won't tell my wife" or "I won't tell my son or my daughter, I'll keep it to myself" or "I'll take care of it all by myself".

We are all part of a Oneness, like a tapestry of life woven so tightly that you cannot keep it to yourself. You can only face with courage the form of change that comes to you. As you face life with strength, remember constantly that you are Spirit, and that you are not this physical body. When terminal illness comes to a physical form, then more than any other time we have to remember that "I am not a man of earth, I am a man of God, I am Spirit". With the dropping away of the worn out vehicle, the spiritual being is set free! And freedom is what life is all about.

Marian

And in Conclusion

As the final message came through I felt a definite change in the usually electro-magnetic charged atmosphere around me. Whenever I had written in the past, a sense of light, peace and a highly charged vibration was present.

As the last word flowed onto the paper, I felt, a definite withdrawal of that energy. Feeling neither sad nor happy, I was in an anti-climactic state. I knew that the process, or "mission" was over.

And so, dear readers, this small offering of our epic of life after death draws to an end. Perhaps a few glimpses beyond the veil have been gleaned, and this wondrous dance called life goes on and on and on!

In sharing these communications, the love as well as the pain, it may help you to understand **we never die, we only change**.

May you always know that love never dies! Just as Life never ends. We truly are forever! And the dance goes on!

In Blessed Lovelight
Marian Young Starnes

REFLECTIONS
REFLECTIONS
FROM SPIRIT

Questions & Insights

into the art of

Living

and

Dying

Introduction to Reflections from Spirit

For over twenty-seven years hundreds of letters have been sent to me, asking many questions about life, death, dreams, conflicts, etc. In an effort to try and answer as many questions as possible, a column called *"Reflections from Spirit"* was created in the early seventies and published in *Crystals of Light*, a quarterly newsletter, published by The Brigade of Light Ministries.

In this portion of the book, I am sharing a cross section of those inquiries and my published responses.

Looking back over the many questions from seekers on the path, I found today, as it was in the beginning, the answers have always remained the same.

Be the best person you can be.

Love God, family, friends, enemies, nature, challenges as well as victories, self, and the gift of life!

Tomorrow is another day, another opportunity to pick myself up, shake off my victim consciousness and begin again!

Never ever give up! Life is for living, learning and loving! There is never an obstacle or challenge that doing the loving thing won't be the right action.

Marian

Q. *So many predictions have been made by various channels about extraordinary numbers of deaths in the immediate future. Would you comment on this, please?*

A. There is *NO* death! There is only an entrance into greater, fuller Life! The much dreaded death process doesn't really exist. It is only liberation from the bondage of flesh, in order to allow the individual to move into a richer, more rewarding existence. Since we are Spirit there can not be a non-existence (death) for any of us. Death is merely a continuation of the living process, and a vital portion of one's own consciousness and evolvement.

What does it matter which "room" we dwell in? Death, if we could but realize it, is one of our most important activities! We've all been born many times; we've experienced death many times. And we're still here, fully conscious on our spiritual journey. *Death is simply a matter of consciousness!*

Yes, many Light bearers and those earthbound (through selfish, cruel, wicked and materialistic living), will go through the Liberation Gateway called Death. Many Light bearers will cross over to *help* the great number of shocked and confused souls crossing over in fear. Yet it matters not which plane we dwell on, as long as we are choosing to serve the Creator.

With the Higher Frequency of the unfolding 5th dimensional energies, many earthbound souls will choose to leave, rather than make the necessary changes being presented to humankind right now.

As long as one's consciousness identifies with the *physical* aspect of self, death will hold its ancient terror. But, as soon as you know yourself as *Spirit*, death no longer is something to be dreaded. It becomes just another step along the way of Life.

It has been written by several that the earth is overpopulated, and Earth mother will send forth eruptions and catastrophes to offer many souls the opportunity to leave. This is an interesting concept, based upon the great need to restore balance between humanity and environment and resources. Since I do not have a viewing window into future events, I would hesitate to speak this as a future prediction. However, it wouldn't surprise me.

Whether or not great numbers of people go though the death process in the near future isn't really the issue. The foremost item of business before us is not "what if..." but to learn that dying is not an *end*, but instead a new *beginning*. Death, in truth, is merely an entry into an interval of healing and restoration, until the soul has the need to venture forth in another body, time and place.

So many in fear, desperately pray for "divine intervention" or for "space brothers" to avert cataclysmic actions on the earth. Because of our Free Will, *it is not theirs to change*, but rather to lead us gently through the period of chaos and change upon the earth. A true spiritual seeker knows there must be change in order for all to grow into greater awareness of their own divine nature. I refer you to the 91st Psalm, which is one of the greatest protection mantras ever given to humanity.

Do not dwell in fear upon predictions of terrible things that "might happen". Rather, stand steadfast in love and faith and know that you are loved and protected in the best and worst of times. ✺

Q. *Every time I see a paper these days, I read about destruction from tornadoes, cyclones, hurricanes or other "killer winds". Why are we experiencing so many of these things at this time?*

A. These winds are acting out the *mental* and *emotional* creation of man! As long as the human mind rages and storms, so, also will the air elements rage and storm. The killer winds will end when man learns to control his thoughts and feelings.

In spiritual symbology, winds indicate cleansing set into motion by the Masters. Stormy winds indicate mass cleansing of astral currents, which are loaded with guilt, fear and anger. Cold, stormy winds indicate the death of our unfounded false beliefs and our false need to judge one another.

The terrible storms can only end when humanity quits miscreating things like ugliness, fear, hate and war. When the human condition creates in gentleness and beauty, then the air elements will return to us as gentle, soothing zephyr winds that cool, cleanse and comfort. Until that time, the elements can only return our violent thoughts and feelings to us, and the "killer winds" will continue to rage.

You must remember that all thoughts and energies go in a circle. What we send out, we get back, often intensified many fold. Nature mirrors Man's emotions. We send out raging thoughts. We get back raging, destructive winds! When, I wonder, will we ever learn that we are constantly creating our reality? ✵

Q. *Everywhere I turn, I read and hear about how awful the late 90's are going to be for planet earth and mankind in general. I'm frightened and confused. How do you view the upcoming years?*

A. I make a point of not trying to view a year, or a month, or even a week in advance. If we are strong in our faith and *living in harmony with Life*, according to Divine and Holy Law, we know there is a far greater law than *Karma*. That is *The Law of Grace* which takes each individual through the very "eye of the storm", without harm!

That things are changing rapidly here on earth cannot be denied by even the most dense ego. Change is definitely needed, now! This very day an estimated 193,000,000 people are hungry and suffering from malnutrition. Over forty wars or armed conflicts are taking place upon this planet. Crime is rising, selfishness is rampant, and anger rules supreme. Fear is everywhere. Judgments against one another has become our way of life. The people are arming themselves with lethal weapons, against each other. Assassination has become an everyday occurrence. Children can no longer play safely in their innocence, because perverts and kidnappers stalk the land. Gold is king, and silver its consort! Churches are bombed, and synagogues are defiled. Our prisons are cesspools of perversion and violence. Mental institutions are so full that it is humanly impossible to effectively rehabilitate, so they can only contain the patients.

Greed and contempt for the Laws of Love and sharing with one another have become a way of Life! This is what we, the race of Man have created for ourselves and our heirs! A planet so steeped in hatred that it is a barren wasteland. Yes, change is coming, and not a minute too soon!

God will not be mocked! Simple Laws of Love and obedience have been given to guide mankind through it's growing pains. The karmic *Law of Return* brings back to us now the fruits of our own bitter seeds. And the prophets speak of doom, destruction and days of darkness. They are sent by the Creator to try to *shock* us into turning back toward the healing, loving Laws of Life, before we actually succeed in destroying ourselves.

Yes, I see these things, and my heart is heavy, and I weep in the night for the sorrows man has drawn to himself. We pray for God's help and Light. Yet, often when Great Souls *try* to be born into the earth, in order to be healers, teachers, and way-showers, the potential mothers opt again and again for abortion, and no suitable vehicles (bodies) are available. As a result the help and Light we pray for cannot come to us, because we refuse entrance into our world of the very ones that could bring it! As a result of abortion, alone, over half of the Light has been turned back!

So, here we are, in the throes of this last decade of the twentieth century which was spawned out of old concepts, beliefs, and patterns. Dressed in the dirty, ragged garments of our distorted consciousness, we plead for new robes and new shoes. Tired and weary from the heavy cross of shame that we have built, we ask for succor and for Light. And our world trembles and moves beneath our feet, as the planet itself tries to throw off the heavy burden of our wrong doings! Where do we go from here?

My friend, there is a way out! The Law of Grace is still there, waiting for the return of the prodigal! Lay down your weapons of anger, fear, hate, greed, selfishness, lust and judgments! Stand before your own indwelling God Presence, and pledge yourself to "fight no more forever"! Draw the pink love energy of the Comfort Flame around yourself and "Be Still and Know that I Am God"!

Forgive yourself, and everyone else, wherever they may be and *leave their judgments to God*! Reach out in love and sweet peace to bless all life! Let no more the curse fall from your lips;   speak Love, instead!

The twenty-third Psalm has become my anchor, and God, alone has power in my life. I see the 90's as a decade of *opportunity*, a chance to correct the wrongful patterns, and to cast off the ragged garments of the past, a new beginning as we approach the 21st century.

The Lord is my shepherd! I shall never want again. Blessed be the name of the Lord. ✸

Q. *What do you see in regard to all the predictions of earth changes, famine, war, etc.?*

A. Change will always be with us, for only through change can new patterns come forth. So many people have prayed for peace and sacrificed for it, that I feel the predicted World War III will not come about. Minor wars and skirmishes will erupt until all people long for peace, but major nuclear holocaust seems to have been averted for the time being. Prayer does, indeed, work!

I feel many of the predicted earth changes have been "slowed down", and we have a little more time than originally thought. As we become more loving custodians of the earth, her resources and our environment, perhaps it won't be necessary that we experience such radical and violent changes. As we treat the earth and all portions of life, minerals, plants, animals, humans, seen and unseen forces, with love, our newly awakening love will spread around the world as a healing balm. Perhaps, then, perfection will once more come about here on this blessed planet!

Instead of using your precious energies "waiting" for the predicted disaster, why don't you greet every day as a wonderful opportunity to create harmony and beauty in your own little part of the universe? One step at a time, as co-creators with God, perhaps our beautiful planet will be saved from the darkness *we* have miscreated.

After all, *this* day is what really counts, isn't it? Live it fully and peacefully! ☀

Q. *Overall, how do you view this final decade of the twentieth century?*

A. I see the 90's as a glorious opportunity to correct a lot of our past mistakes. A time when individuals and nations throw off the yoke of bondage and enslavement, whether it is an ideology, government, or addiction. I believe we will, after much trial and error in the early part of the decade, find ourselves making definite efforts to return to a God Consciousness. In fact, I *see the nineties as a worldwide return to the sacred*. Prayer will once more be "in", and larger numbers of people will seek to follow a more giving, caring, sharing and loving path.

In the 80's worldwide social problems loomed up everywhere. Life-threatening diseases touched nearly every community, and violence ran rampant. The environment, now poisoned and contaminated by our ignorance and misuse of resources, screamed out for healing! The mass mind slowly began to realize change MUST come about, if we are to survive.

Sexual perversions, drugs, alcohol, and violence moved into our midst, and became *every* human's business. As we cried out in alarm, "My God, what is happening to us", a deep desire for peace, purity and goodness was awakened.

I believe that in the awakening we will see the decade of the 90's as a door to a more *elevated consciousness*, and a deep desire for a return to God will spring forth. I believe the 90's will bring a swift move toward world peace and unity between peoples, but not without much pain and hardship for all.

The early part of the decade will be stressful and tumultuous as the winds of change blow away the old patterns of the past. But, toward the end of the decade, great strides will be made toward a more peaceful coexistence as we try to become more godly. ☀

Q. *Why are there so many natural disasters right now, such as storms, floods and earthquakes?*

A. This is a time of great cleansing, as the Earth shakes off the ugliness and darkness that we have miscreated by our angers, fears, hate, greed and selfishness. This is truly, the Day of Purification, and no part of the earth can escape. *Change is here now!* There will continue to be disasters of these natures until we learn we need each other, and that we are our Brother's keepers. Until we learn to be loving and true stewards of our environment and the earth, we will experience Nature in rebellion against our selfishness! Even the elements of weather are in revolt against the imbalance. It will end when we turn our attention back toward the Creator, and our hearts in loving kindness toward one another!

Q. *Was the earthquake in California a terrible karma because of their sinful ways?*

A. Not at all!!! Race consciousness karma more than personal karma is being played our on this particular stage. The race of Man, as a whole, has created a great thought form of dark energy, or as many call it, sinfulness. The world operates in perfect balance when the energy is loving, caring, kind and gentle. But when the human condition is steeped in greed, hate, resentment, rage and depravity, the balance or harmony is lost. Then things get "tipped upside down". This is to awaken us to the need to create a different kind of energy if we want beauty, peace and harmony. The future of our world is up to us! If we change, it will change.

Q. *Why did God let all those poor people die and suffer from that release of poisonous gas in India a few years ago? Why do these things happen?*

A.   Let's be very clear about one thing, *God did not cause this to happen,* we did! We are constantly creating chaos in our world, through our misuse of the Divine Laws of the Universe. Ignorance of these Laws and/or disobedience to them fills our world with negative, destructive patterns. As long as we insist on living in a chemical world, developing toxins and poisons, these kinds of tragedies will take place. What happened in India is the out picturing of the greed and the disregard that man has for the purity of our environment and planet, as well as our disregard for one another!

The farther we drift from a personal, loving relationship with our Creator, the more we will become *masters of chaos.* Our fears and angers cause us to search for more ways to kill, conquer and destroy one another, even though God clearly gives us Laws of Love and Peace. We've drifted far away from the harmonious relationship we once had with Nature. Now our greed and fear causes us to search for more poisons and chemicals to try to restore balance to our world, not by loving cooperation, but by force! The thought forms of poisons become monstrous until, at last, in some weakened place, they burst forth as a catastrophe into the outer world. As long as we insist on chemicals and toxins being part of our world, the "thought patterns" of death and destruction will continue to grow. Periodically they will erupt and spew out their deadly actions upon the world that gave them life. This is what happened in India.

All people are one in spirit, and therefore part of race and planetary karma. Those who suffered were acting within the framework of racial and planetary karma, rather than their own individual patterns. Truly we are our brothers' keeper for when we create chaos, any part of the planet may be the recipient of the destructive results.

As long as we are blind to Nature as an integral part of our world, and ignore its need to be nurtured, we'll be dependent on chemicals. When we learn to cooperate with and love nature, pesticides won't be necessary, for plagues of harmful insects will no longer be manifesting in our world. Loving reverence for Life, and joyous cooperation with all parts of God's creation restores harmony and order. Living in ignorance with arrogant disregard for Life causes plagues, insects, spoilage and death. So out of our lack of love for life we've brought forth those negative forms that caused us to seek chemicals, poisons and toxic materials as our solution. Chemicals are not the solution. ***Love is the only answer that works.*** Anything other than love is merely falsehood trying to correct the already existing errors that we've created.

Perhaps India will cause us to stop and re-evaluate our priorities, and the course we've set for ourselves. ✺

Q. *How does that relate to the millions starving in Africa and all the other deprived parts of the world?*

A. As long as man hoards food, fearful that he won't have enough for himself tomorrow, patterns of hunger will develop. Denying food to the less fortunate, and refusing to share our good with one another creates thought forms of hunger and starvation! Greed and hate are terrible bedfellows, and the patterns they leave behind them can only lead to death.

Life is sharing, giving, and blessing. Death is grasping, hoarding, and cursing. We're blind to the needs of our fellow man, and out of our blindness comes the terrible patterns being played out all over the world. Nature follows man's example, for man has dominion over the earth. As the milk of human kindness dries up in the human breast, so do the life giving rains of nature dry up. Nature is simply following man's pattern. When man closes himself away from Life and caring, he becomes barren and empty. Nature, following this pattern, recreates that barrenness through drought and empty fields! This then leaves the people to struggle with lack, deprivation and hunger. ✺

Q.   *When does the soul actually enter the body?*

A.   There are three distinct steps or procedures involved in the process of bringing forth new life in the miracle or birth:

In the first stage, from conception to the moment of the first movement, the Guardian Angel of the incoming soul and a Body Elemental are in charge of creating the vehicle or body. They are the cosmic contractors building the appropriate form. During this period, the soul may "oversee" the construction, but it does not take possession of the body.

The second stage begins with the first movement which occurs when the subconscious mind joins the Guardian Angel and Body Elemental. Now feelings and thoughts begin to be stored in the cell memory.

The last stage occurs at the moment of birth, at which time the Holy Spirit must breathe in the breath of Life, and at that moment the incoming soul takes charge of the body. The Soul then has the use of the vehicle until the Holy Spirit takes back that breath of Life at the moment called death.

In summation, the incoming soul contracts for a body, with certain specifications as to gender, race, shape, condition, etc. The Body Elemental builds according to the contract. The soul oversees, or keeps an eye on the body as it is forming. But it is a "turn-key" job. The soul does not take possession until the construction is complete.

Only the Holy Spirit can breathe a soul (Life) into a body vehicle. Only the Holy Spirit can disconnect the soul at death. ✸

Q. *What should we do about abortion? With so many unwanted pregnancies, what is the spiritual solution?*

A.   Well, the answer is *not another law*, permitting or outlawing abortion. *Abortion is not the problem*! It is a *symptom* of a far greater issue. That issue is our failure to educate children to revere their bodies and to teach the sacredness of the sexual act. Parenting skills should be our very first educational priority, taught from kindergarten through high school. Procreation should be considered as sacred as prayer, meditation and holy service! When we, as the human race, learn to treat our sexuality as a sacred trust, and learn the full responsibility of becoming sexually active, we will take a giant step beyond needing abortion laws. Otherwise, people who live in their sexual senses and not in spiritual responsibility, will continue to perpetuate the present out of control condition. Irresponsible sexual practices will continue to cause far too many pregnancies, and thus the ever present issue of abortion.

Not more laws! Educate! Educate! Educate! ☀

Q.   *Is there karma connected with organ donations?*

A.   The soul records are stored in the heart, eyes, and blood. The recipient of any of these does "buy into" the karma of the donor. However, the *motive* to do a loving, life-prolonging act, such as donation of an organ or blood, often far out-weighs the connected karma, and an act of Grace balances out whatever karmic residue was involved. In the end, it is not the action of organ donation that really counts, it is the motivation. It is always the feeling and motive that determines the karma.

Q.   *What can I do when others around me are negative, and constantly "programming" me with suggestions of lack, failure, etc.?*

A.   That is their problem, not yours. Do not accept their thoughts and words as your own. You cannot serve two masters! When you give credence or power to another person, you recognize them as your master. A false God! To negative suggestions from others, say: "*I Am* the Presence, annulling all of this, so it cannot affect me, my home, or my world. It has no power over me"! It is the easiest thing in the world to consciously dissipate something that is voiced in your presence. Simply state: " *I Am* the only Presence acting here" or "This is *not* my Truth"!

    To anything you do not wish to accept or to continue, say: "Through the Presence that *I Am*, this (situation) shall cease, now and forever"! Say it with conviction, and mean it!

    Try to realize the Limitless Power at your command! Believe it! Use it! The Truth, indeed, will set you free!

Q. *I have read about the Space Brothers' plans for the evacuation of planet earth. It all sounds so awful and fearsome. What should I do now?*

A.   When you board a plane, the attendant gives you evacuation instructions. You don't then, sit there waiting for the plane to crash. You file the information away, "just in case", and continue on to your destination, secure in the knowledge that if disaster comes, there is a way out. So it is with this kind of information. It's comforting to know there is help available should the situation become critical, but I absolutely refuse to live in a world of fear, waiting for the end. Instead, I will live each day as richly loving, and positive as possible, in full faith of God's promise of Life!

What should you do now? Know yourself and love your neighbor, forgive your enemies and reach out in gentle, compassionate love to all you meet. Fear not what "might" happen tomorrow, but stand strong in faith today! Love and serve and bless all, to the best of your ability. If you "fall down in faith" get back up, dust yourself off, and love again! Bless Life, and perhaps we won't need to "evacuate", because God's perfect plan will begin to work out for all of us! ✺

Q. *What can I do to help the Earth?*

A. *Nothing! The Earth* is Divine Principle, divine manifestation under the direct control, healing, and balancing of the Angelic Hosts, spiritual hierarchy and those Divine Beings that are ahead of us in their evolution. *The World* is man's creation and is constantly being changed, rearranged, destroyed, as man comes into different areas of awareness. The World must always be destroyed to make way for new ideas and forms. The Earth is eternal and endures infinitely.

As we change our consciousness, our world changes and disappears to make way for new growth. Civilizations rise and fall. Political, economic, educational and social structures emerge, are used, and then fall away, always making way for new unfolding forms. The World, as we know it, will be destroyed, which means we will change our conscious awareness of our worldly creation. The World will drop away, as it is dropping away right now. The cataclysmic action we are seeing is part of this. We are seeing nations crumble, and other nations rise. We are seeing things change. We are seeing the changing of consciousness, the changing of the illusion, the dispelling of the darkness of the World.

Let your work be for the healing and balancing of our world. Worry not about the Earth. The Earth is Divine and will last long after the last one of mankind has walked through the door and has risen up into the next dimension. It will still be here, ready to nurture the next evolution. The reality is the Earth. The illusion is the World. We operate in the illusion. *The Earth is the Divine Principle* presented to mankind so that we might create a World. ☀

Q. *What can I do to help Mankind?*

A.   The greatest service you can possibly render to your fellowman is to work on yourself! Work on your attitudes and relationships. Learn compassion, mercy, tolerance and forgiveness! Live in harmony with Life and let peace go forth from you in all of your affairs. Draw a little closer to the Father and live in His love-light. Let your hand reach out in brotherhood. Center yourself and be at peace. As you raise your consciousness, you raise all of mankind, for we are, truly, One in Spirit. ☀

Q. *I seem to have a lot of heavy "bad" karma this lifetime. What can I do to "lighten the load"?*

A.   Get busy doing all that you can to ease the burden for someone else! Share and serve, and praise the Creator for the opportunity to meet so many situations that give you a chance to learn. Pay off bad karma by creating good! Don't concern yourself with "how much" or "why". In selfless, loving service to others you will begin to experience release (Grace) from the troublesome seeds of your past. ☀

Q. *Nothing ever seems to go smoothly in my life. Why?*

A. We get exactly what we need. Friction acts like a prod to get us moving and working. Without the friction we'd stop evolving.

If things are going too smoothly, you're probably not learning anything. That harmonious period is reward time, like a sabbath or rest period, a time to feel gratitude and thanks. You rest awhile, and then comes the conflict, problem or friction, and you "get back into the game of Life", overcoming, learning, growing. Don't curse the strife, my dear, instead bless it, for it means you're "still in the game" and no doubt, learning far more than you did during the period of serenity.

Q. *Does that mean there will always be friction?*

A. Not at all. As we grow, learning to live in harmony with the dynamic cosmic laws of Life, we no longer need the friction. When we are applying the truth in all of our affairs, we are close to receiving our "master's degree" and no longer need the conflict in order to grow. But until we are willing to surrender our ego and will completely to Divine Will we will continue to meet conflict and friction. What you bless in Life will come back to enrich and bless you; resist and curse it, and it will keep on knocking you down until the lesson is finally learned. And that choice is always yours!

Q. *What is that lesson we're all struggling to learn?*

A. Simple. Love! God is Love. Life is Love. I am Love. You are Love. In the beginning the Word was Love, which is Life and Light. Yet we spend many lifetimes trying to change that law to fit our own disobedient concept of God. We are constantly trying to create God in our own image and our image is always changing as we are evolving. So we deny or curse God because It does not fulfill our needs in the moment. We struggle, and hate and connive to make God into something that is not only untrue, but impossible. Our lives continue to be unhappy, limited, and conflicted because we're not yet willing to accept the simplest, purest Truth, Love. ☼

Q. *Then when does the unhappiness end or does it ever?*

A. When we have learned to love and be loved. When we stop hating, lying, possessing, and judging one another, and surrender to the sweet harmony of God's pure love. Then our heaven on earth really begins and our world radiates joy and light, instead of sorrow and darkness. When does it end? Dear one, only you can answer that. Whenever you are ready to "let go and let God" your unhappiness will be transformed into a joy and serenity such as you have never experienced before. ☼

Q. *I long for God. In what direction should I be looking?*

A. Look upward for Light, inward for serenity and comfort, outward for places to serve and people to love. And look downward in humble gratitude for the very ground you stand upon. Bless the earth that nurtures you. All is God. Look in all directions! ☀

Q. *Why is there always so much friction everywhere? When will it stop?*

A. Why? Because we're learning! When will it stop? When you stop looking outside yourself. The day you stop looking outside yourself and stop pointing your fingers at other people and paying attention to what they're doing, the day you stop fighting, then the Angel of the Lord really goes before you and rolls away the obstacles. We have friction because that's how we learn. I used to think that it was some kind of heavy duty trip that God had put on me. I didn't know that it was just *increased opportunities* for me to learn. And I'm doing the best that I can, day by day. The friction will stop when we stop. When we stop looking outside ourselves, blaming others, serving the false God of fear, and the false God of anger, and the false god of guilt. If one doesn't get you, the other one will. Sometimes they gang up and all three pile up on you. But the day you stop paying homage to these three and say, "No! No more! You have no power over me! Only God (all good) is acting in my life". The day you stop hating yourself, and the day you stop putting yourself down, the day you dare to declare peace for yourself, it will be over and you'll go home. ☀

Q.   *Several of us meet once a week in my home to meditate and discuss spiritual matters. What should I do to prepare our meeting place for these gatherings?*

A.   No set formula, ritual, or arrangement of furniture makes one place better than another. In inspirational work it is not the house, furniture, candles, incense, etc., that attracts Light. It is the serenity, devoutness and sincerity that inspires people to seek these meetings. Those who choose to attend are drawn there by the Consciousness of Truth. They come to your house to enter a temple of God; to share the inspirational energies of spirituality. Divine Consciousness enfolds all those who attend the meetings. As each one tunes into that consciousness, blessings of healing, peace, balance and upliftment are drawn into the circle. Each one receives according to their willingness to believe and accept.

Know ye not that *you* are the temple of God? And that where you are is holy ground, for God's temples stand upon His essence of holiness? Therefore, the home you have opened up to God's work in the outer form, is already a sacred place, by your own God Presence within! Be still and know that I Am God. ☀

Q.   *I've become very aware of colors since I consciously started on my quest. Some mornings I change my clothes several times, until I get the "right" color for the day. I need to know, do colors really have any special spiritual significance?*

A.   Indeed they do! Your own soul will lead you to the colors most needed at your level of awareness. Just as the beautiful colors in a rainbow strike a cord of joy and hope within the beholder, so do all colors resonate for each of us. (Often when I am tired, I will choose to wear a bright red blouse or jacket, as a "color pick me up").

Each color vibrates at a different frequency. Intuitively we will seek the vibration that best fits our pattern. As we grow spiritually our color selections often change tremendously. I have listed below a sampling of colors and their corresponding significance.

Blue: Calmness, spiritual awareness, devotion, honesty, faith, power, serenity, cooperation and harmony.

Yellow/Gold: Intelligence, illumination, mental awareness, joy, happiness, well-being, laughter and innocence.

Pink/Rose: Love, compassion, mercy, devotion, responsibility, tenderness, helpfulness, caring and friendship.

White: Purity, guilelessness, goodness, cleanliness, God awareness, openness, Christ-like, without fear or anger.

Green: Balance, healing, harmony, teaching, science, abundance, understanding and Life.

Red: Vital force, physical energies, courage, strength, pure unadulterated love, action, fast moving, an activator, enthusiasm.

Orange: Vital energy with wisdom, inventiveness, mental creativity, clarity, intelligent power, originality and astuteness, action with wisdom.

Violet/Purple: Spiritual transformation, dedication to good, transmutation, ceremonial "magic", changing the dross to gold, deep spirituality, freedom, inner peace.

Black: Hides and veils. People often wear black as a mask, covering their true selves, dense and slow moving, often considered the color of introspection.

Silver: Illumination, spiritual power and connectedness to God, expansive and far reaching.

Rainbows: Promise, hope, the full spectrum of all of the qualities of all of the colors, God.

Brown/Tan: Neutral, materialistic, earthy, grounded in the physical world, stable.

These are general indicators. Every emotion and thought disturbs, adds to or "smudges" the true essence of a color. General knowledge of the frequency of each color can help us in our day to day choices.

Example: A hyperactive child would be further agitated in a room with alot of red. A blue or green room would lend more calming effects to the situation.

Q.   *I've studied, meditated and prayed to try to find the path to God.   I should be joyous and peaceful; instead I am stressed, emotional and easily angered.   What am I doing wrong?*

A.   Fear and unforgiven things from the past block our way completely. Like a "Beware of fallen rock" sign on the highway, fear and lack of forgiveness stop us dead in our tracks, and we can't go on until both have been resolved through understanding, love and faith.

Fear is separation from God. When we are out of the divine flow, the soul fears that it is threatened or lost. As the fear grows, the Inner Light dims, and we stray farther and farther from the sense of our own divinity. We start to "fall out of love" and begin to accuse, suspect or blame others for our unhappiness.

We are lost in our feelings of inadequacy, and the darkness grows stronger, as we live less and less in the peace and joy of belief in the Light. Our actions become irrational, revenge-oriented, and attacking as the soul struggles to survive. As fear and anger grow, we no longer see good (God) in others, and they become potential threats or enemies.

If you would know Light, cast into the Light all fears, angers, judgments and unforgiven situations. As you release these things into the healing Light of the Christ, peace and joy, and a sense of well being will once more flood your being. You will once again view others in love instead of hate and fear.

"I release all of my past, fears, angers and judgments into the Light! I Am a Child of Light! I Am healed by the Light! I Am surrounded by the pure, white Light of the Christ, and all is well in my Life! Amen". ✹

Q.   *Would you say something about appearances?*

A.   We tend to look with these all too human eyes and see the outer appearance of people and situations, without taking time to look beyond to the true nature of things, which is Spirit. Just as you can't know what is in my heart, I cannot know what motivates you. We forget (if we ever really knew) that we all are spiritual beings learning, growing, hurting, loving, and at last, overcoming our human weaknesses. We see a man and judge him "good" or "bad" on the basis of what he *appears* to be, without knowledge of his *true* nature or purpose. We forget that God is constantly manifesting through all of the human creations, therefore that man we judge might just be one who has come to teach us *not* to judge. When we begin to look with eyes of love and tolerance at ourselves, then we are ready to see *beyond* the appearance to what truly is in others. And another "false god" falls by the wayside! ☀

Q. *What is sin?*

A.   The only real sin on this plane is *ignorance*! It is ignorance of the Divine Principle. It is ignorance of the power of the mind. It is ignorance of the qualities of Love. It is ignorance of the tremendous expansive power of God. It is ignorance of our role as part of a Universal Whole. *The only sin is ignorance*. And this is "the sin against the Holy Spirit".

It is ignorance that causes us to fear another part of life. We fear other races or nations. One political group fears another, straights fear gays, men fear women and vice versa, and the list goes on and on. *It is ignorance of who we really are.*

When you act in harmony with Life in the Divine Flow, you are moving away from sin and you are entering into the Creative Path of experiencing and growing. By learning and remembering who you are and how you fit in the grand scheme of things, you are learning to move in harmony with Life.

That's all that "sin" is. The church has taken sin and hung it around our necks like an albatross, when in truth our sin is our ignorance. And the overcoming of the sin is when we begin to remember and recall who we truly are, our Divine Self. As we remember, and yet continue to do the same old things, it is still not sin, it is our mistakes and our errors and our obstacles that we have to overcome. Is it any wonder, then, that so many spiritually minded people now call sin "self imposed nonsense". ✺

Q. *Lately I've been feeling overwhelmed by all the stuff I seem to have accumulated over the years. It makes me feel disorganized and boxed in, but I don't know what to do about it. Any suggestions?*

A. One of the great lessons we have come to learn is that of Order. Order in our thoughts, in the places where we live and work, in our cars, and in our relationships. No matter how much we learn metaphysically, until we have *order* in our lives, we'll continue to feel scattered.

It's hard to plant orderly seeds of harmony and beauty around us when our closets are filled with junk, the dressers are crammed with stuff that's been there for years, trash is piled sky-high and you can't walk through the garage without running into more junk! And, we're afraid to open the glove compartment of the car for fear we'll never get it closed again. You aren't alone with your dilemma! We've all experienced the same thing.

The way to start on the Path of Light is *clean up where you live!* Not only endeavor to make yourself as attractive as you can, but do the same for your surroundings. Throw away the "stuff" of the past. Clean up! Clear out! Get rid or the useless, worn out things as well as the worn out ideas of the past!

No one ever planted a rose garden without cleaning up the space first. We need to clean up our space, create a vacuum and make room for beauty and order to come into our lives. ✺

Q. *I've heard you talk about freedom, but I don't know how to find it. Does it mean I should get a divorce, since my marriage isn't very happy? What should I do first?*

A. The first thing you do toward claiming your freedom is learn how to love yourself. It doesn't mean you file for a divorce or quit your job. To *claim* your freedom, you must first realize that *you deserve it!*

You don't have to take the garbage that the world dishes up. You're not helpless! You are created in the image of God. You are empowered by the Holy Spirit, and you always have been. You just forgot and got trapped in the dark creation of your ignorance.

You can have whatever kind of day you want. If you get up, and then moan "I feel miserable and it's going to be a rotten day", *that is your creation.* If you want to feel happy, light hearted, optimistic, or you want to work or you don't want to work, it all is your *choice.* To be free, you need to understand and live by the spiritual principles of Love.

You need to learn to love yourself enough to stop running away from your emptiness. ***Stop complaining.*** *Start loving, and giving and sharing.* And give the first gift to yourself, the gift of *allowing* yourself to be happy. Then you've got something to give to someone else. You can't love anyone until you start loving who you are. And you certainly can't love God if you despise His finest creation, which happens to be you! *You are the greatest miracle in the universe.* You are the Divine child. The Path of Freedom begins the day you discover you! ✹

Q. *I can hardly force myself to go to work each day, and I frequently stay home. But need I the money, and so I must work. What can I do?*

A. Find a job doing something you *like* doing, and do it with joy. It looks like you stay in a job you hate because of money. That is *not* a good reason to take a job. When you are unhappy on a job, staying there only because of money, everyone loses, including you, through the fear and unhappiness you create. Bless the present job, and then affirm (pray) "Infinite Spirit, lead me now to the wonderful work that is mine by Divine Right, with the right people, right conditions and right pay, In God's own wonderful way"! ☀

Q. *What does forgiveness really mean?*

A. Forgiveness means to give something for, to replace or give something in place of. When we learn to let go of yesterday and all past relationships, looking not backwards but being in the NOW, we are in a state of forgiveness. We are filling our hearts with new ideas, thoughts and feelings, and not letting it be poisoned by hates, resentments and fears of the past. Thus we give up the old worn out things, replacing them with a new, loving state of consciousness. *To forgive is to live. Unforgiveness is to begin to die.* Life is loving inspiring energy lived moment by moment. Therefore in forgiveness we give up the past for the newness and peace of today. ☀

Q. *My life is miserable from all my fears, angers and guilts. Sometimes I feel such a rage, I make myself sick. Then I get afraid and overcome by guilt. Is there anyway out? I feel like I'm in prison!*

A.   Anger and guilt, the inseparable twins of agony, spawned by the demon Fear, will always torture those who are ignorant of their true spiritual nature. Jesus said "The Truth will set you free". May I suggest:

Look at it! Look your fear square in the eye, and know that it is a false god. Take the power away from it. Cast it out! It has absolutely no power over you, if you refuse to give it!

Forgive It! Look back gently and lovingly over your past, and forgive it all, as you also forgive yourself. For you were only learning not failing, and all of those relationships and situations were merely your classroom.

See yourself Divinely! Go to a mirror, and look deeply into your own eyes, and look at God looking back at you. For you are a perfect idea in the Divine Mind of God!

Love it! Love who you are, what you are, where you are, what you are doing, and who you are doing it with! And then love again!

Believe! Read again the 23rd Psalm, and the 91st Psalm, and pray the Lord's Prayer for strength.

Learn!   Read *Love Is Letting Go Of Fear*
                                                  by Gerald Jampolsky

Accept! And affirm "I Am *MY* Father's very beloved child. His Love and Grace bless me *NOW.* Free me forever from my demons of fear and anger. I am filled with peace and harmony, and it is very,very good! Thank you, Father, for my freedom." ☀

Q. *What is a mantra? Do I need one? Where do I get the right one for me?*

A. A mantra is the sounding, repeatedly, of a word or words to help dissolve tension, fear and karma. Each word contains vibrations of Light energies that are activated when the word is spoken prayerfully. Voiced with love and faith, the sacred mantra becomes a tool of freedom.

No, you don't need one, but it certainly speeds up the process of evolution if sacred words are spoken reverently and frequently.

A teacher or guru may give you a mantra, but your own soul is more likely to do so. As a Light statement repeats itself in your mind, it becomes your personal mantra, your prayer of self.

"I Am Light" or "I Am Love" are very simple, but powerful mantras. Repeat them many times a day, upon arising, at noontime, in the evening, and whenever you are under stress. Repetitive soundings penetrate the subconscious mind, and as it begins to believe you really are Light, then joy and peace permeate the consciousness. Soon, from the place of peace and serenity you begin making clearer decisions and choices. As clear thinking emerges, dark fears and angers fade away to allow your beautiful Inner Christ Child to emerge. ☀

Q. *Is my life predestined? Do I really have any choices in my life?*

A. For all of you who think your destiny is set, and that you are destined to be where you are now for the rest of your life, I have one answer. NO! It is not the truth!

The page of tomorrow is not yet written for a single one of us. Every individual writes their own script. We carry our own pen of Life, and we dip it into the wellspring of our desires and understanding, and write the script day by day!

It's our story. It can be a horror tale filled with shock and fear. It can be a comedy, a mystery, a love story, or a rambling pointless hodge podge of foolishness. But you can be sure of one thing. God *isn't writing it, we are*!

The Creator gave you the pen and the paper called Life, and said "Go write your own play, and I will allow you to star in it"! And with that sent you forth with the gift of free will to create your own reality.

There's only one thing you can dip the pen into if you're going to live in joy and peace. It must be written in love, tolerance and forgiveness! If your pen is dipped in greed, fear, anger and guilt, your story will be one of sorrow and bitterness. Until we learn to write only in love, the same old dark tale repeats over and over.

What is your story? Is it a tale of woe? Or is it a cosmic love story? Just be assured, neither is predetermined. Each is created moment by moment, by you the author of your life experiences. ✺

Q. *What do you think about what we're being shown in movies such as "Ghost", and other films like that which seem to be so popular at this time?*

A. I feel all of the "windows of heaven" are flung open and the mysteries of Life and death are no longer hidden and secret. I am so very happy movies such as these are now available to the masses. Seeds are being planted to make even the most earthbound soul start to think about something better, that life does continue after death. Hooray for Hollywood.

Shirley MacLaine went "out on a limb" and took the whole world with her. "Close Encounters", "E.T." and "Cocoon" took us to the stars. "Ghost" takes us through the veil of fear surrounding the change called Death. All of these have been wonderfully orchestrated by the Angels to awaken Man to his own immortality. All of these are used as door openers into the Realms of Truth which have been closed for too long to the mass mind.

I believe we will see many, many, presentations along these spiritual lines until the knowledge of Light and Truth becomes quite commonplace upon this plane. The seeker then will no longer need to feel isolated and alone in his or her truth. It will have become general knowledge. I believe such public viewings will go far toward removing the aspects of fear and doubt about man's divinity and immortality.

God uses many instruments to awaken us to the way of Love. I think that these movies are just a few of God's special messengers. ✸

Q. *I've heard the name "The Goodly Company" or "The Good Brothers". Who are they? Where do they come from? Why not "The Good Sisters" or are they only men?*

A. At all times there is a group of souls embodied on earth for the express purpose of helping others when they seem to have no place to turn. Some teachers say the Goodly Company numbers three to five hundred individuals both males and females, who unsung and usually unrewarded, act like "Angels" in our lives.

When we are frightened, desperate, alone, and seemingly forsaken, and we cry out to God for help, many times one of these good people just "happens" to appear. What ever is needed, be it a gift, a helping hand, a word of comfort, or an idea, they come to give us a boost at exactly the right crucial moment!

Seldom do these caring souls know they are here on a special mission. Born with compassionate hearts and loving natures, they have an intense desire to relieve human suffering. Even as children they often show tenderness and love, when other children are being cruel to one another.

No prayer for help is left unanswered. When we, in desperation, cry out to God for help the message is usually picked up by one of these "Earth Angels", and they quickly respond! Rarely do they have any conscious memory or knowledge of being an angelic helper. Who knows, *you* might be one of these Good Brothers or Good Sisters! ☼

Q.　*What is the difference between twin flames and soul mates?*

A.　Soulmates, here on earth, are souls who have known and loved each other for many lifetimes. Cell memory of past interactions draws them together, often into very loving relationships. The soul does not forget those that have given love and friendship in the past. Hence, when two people meet, the soul (cell) memory "kicks in", and there is an immediate warmth and trust. The two feel a kindred spirit and mutual affection. This often leads to wonderful working relationships, friendships and even marriage. We can have many soulmates, for in our numerous sojourns upon earth, we have loved many.

Twin flames (twin souls) are the full male and female aspects that came forth from the Great Fire Being, the I Am Presence which is our true identity. Each of us, therefore, has only one twin flame. As a rule, one portion of twin flames will choose to remain in spirit while the other has the earth experience. The one in spirit acts as a guiding light for the embodied one.

When both portions embody simultaneously, it is always for a specific spiritual purpose. The establishing of major Light centers often calls for the full male-female power, and so both will be brought into embodiment for that purpose. Twin flames usually will have a rapport on the mental, emotional, physical and spiritual level, and more than lovers, they will also have tremendous friendships.

As a rule, twin flames do not meet on earth until a specific work for humanity is to be done. They always meet on earth with a sense of mission or purpose. ☀

Q. *How do you keep from being overwhelmed with a desire for vengeance when someone has really wronged you? I meditate and pray, but I keep wanting the one who hurt me to pay. Why shouldn't they hurt when they have hurt me so much?*

A. Under the Laws of Karma, the hurting act brings its own punishment, if not in this time, in another. Who knows where or when the first hurt was created. Because of the *Absolute Law of Return*, no vengeance is needed, for the hurting one has already set in motion their future sorrows. When the Truth student comes to *understand* this great Law, there is no longer a desire for revenge. This is where forgiveness, which comes from understanding, is needed, in order to allow the seeker to move onward and upward.

In Truth no pain or hurt comes to us except that we, ourselves, have created it somewhere in time. Only through love and self-forgiveness can we grow beyond the petty hurts and sorrows. As Jesus said, *"Turn the other cheek and follow thou Me"*! ☀

Q. *Why are some people born with discolorations or birth-marks?*

A.   All birthmarks are recorded in the karmic records of the incarnating one. They come as a reminder of error or omission that hurt others in another life or lives.

Birthmarks upon the hand are like a "string tied around one's finger" to remind one not to be greedy, grasping or taking what does not rightly belong to oneself.

Over-indulgence, vanity and false pride in ones physical beauty in a past life often brings a mark upon the face in the present one.

Birthmarks on the legs or feet may be a reminder to watch or choose careful the pathway to follow. Marks upon the legs also represent a blemish on the will that impedes the soul's progress. It can indicate one who has lagged behind and refuses to progress.

Most birthmarks are chosen by the incoming soul, to help them *remember* what they have come to learn. ✹

Q. *I've read every book on religion, New Age philosophy, healing, crystals and personal power that I can lay my hands on. I've done this for over a decade. I try to practice what I am reading about. Lately I've started feeling depressed and burdened by all this stuff that doesn't seem to work. It's becoming a burden, instead of a joy. It certainly isn't uplifting anymore. What has gone wrong?*

A.   Why don't you stop the intense quest for *information* and take some time off to smell the roses and relax? The Spirit within leads you *gently* into the Cathedral of the Soul, in your heart. It doesn't seek to overload your circuits with more words and techniques! You are experiencing burn out.

Because you've been trying so hard, you forgot how to have fun and to enjoy today. Haven't you heard, the fruits of the spirit are peace, love and joy? Where is your joy? When did you last play? You aren't cramming for finals, my friend you're supposed to be learning how to *live*! Lighten up! Go to a movie. Walk in the park. Play with the dog. Plant a flower. Sing a song. Watch a sunset. Count the stars. Don't you know, darling, the Spirit loves all these little things, for truly, aren't they the real jewels of Life?

Beware of becoming so overloaded with *words* that you can no longer hear the *music*! ☀

Q. *What is "spiritual sanctuary" that you mentioned in a talk recently?*

A. In days of revolution or war, it was the case many times that when someone was escaping from an enemy went to a church or monastery and asked for asylum, the priests took them in, and their pursuers could not follow. It was sanctified ground, and free from the ravishes of war and terrorism.

We are in a time of spiritual and emotional revolt, for the destructive negative energies threaten us every day. When we remember we are, indeed, Christs of God, and that there truly is a sanctified place where we are free from the pettiness, greed, hate, anger and fear that surrounds us, we move into Sanctuary.

In holy silence of meditation, and quiet knowing of God inwardly, we experience freedom from the terrors that mentally pursue us daily. To claim spiritual asylum or sanctuary we need only to take the time to sit in silence (meditation and prayer) and let the threatening outer world come to rest, while the Inner world of peace enfolds us. In that sanctuary we are centered and whole (holy) and strengthened by the Holy Spirit, that we might walk in the world but not be destroyed by it, mentally or emotionally.

Thus each time we go quietly within and experience the sweet peace of the Indwelling Presence of God, we are claiming sanctuary. When this is done daily, consistently, our auric fields will become so harmonized that the outer world can no longer drive us into despair, fear or anger.

Thus, in meditation, I knock upon the temple door and claim spiritual sanctuary, where I am guided, loved, protected and provided with all That I need. In silence "Be still and know that I Am God"! ☼

Q. *I heard you speak once about belief and knowing. I'd like to share what you said with others, but I'm not clear about the differences. Would you comment please?*

A.   Religion, books, legends, parents, peers, and schooling form the basis of our belief system. What you have been taught since childhood has formed your personal beliefs. As social consciousness evolves, and our programming changes our beliefs also change. For myself, I was brought up in Christianity, and the teachings of Jesus the Christ. I had no true understanding of what it all meant. I simply accepted it as truth, as my family before me had done. Blind acceptance without understanding forms most of our beliefs. But, as we grow in understanding, our beliefs change, or even drop away completely.

As a rule, what we *believe*, and what we truly *know* are vastly different. When you have a deep, personal, spiritual experience, belief gives way to profound knowing. A vision, a flash of intuitive insight, a deep meditational union with the God-Self, or a moment of Cosmic Consciousness changes you forever, for now you *know*. And what we know does not change, it just is!

Meditation is the door to finding the Indwelling Spirit that translates belief into knowing. As blind faith (belief) gives way to the spiritual experience, it becomes emblazoned upon your soul. *You now know because you've been there*!

Changing social patterns and religious reforms cannot alter or take one's true knowing away from us. It is a portion of "Eternal Truth" that has become part of us because we have had the very real experience. *Through experience, belief gives way to knowing.* ☀

Q. *What do you consider your greatest opportunity for spiritual growth? Who was your greatest teacher?*

A. My greatest spiritual opportunity was definitely being *born,* and Life, with all its pain and challenges, has been my greatest teacher!

The gift of birth, and the lessons that have followed me these many years is priceless. Every tear, fault, sorrow, humiliation and loss has afforded me the opportunity to grow strong. Life has knocked me down; then given me ways to get back up, brush myself off, and try again! Every mistake was a seed of later knowledge. Every tear cleansed away the darkness until I could finally see the Light. Life *seemed* to be a cruel mistress, but now I know it was all *opportunities of Love*, to aid me in my Godward Path. Just when I felt I couldn't go on another day, a helping hand was always there.

I'm really glad I've had this embodiment. From sorrow, I've learned joy. From fear I've grown into Faith. From anger I've learned how to forgive; from hate I've learned how to Love: and out of the abyss of guilt I've found a great peace! Yes, no doubt about it, Lady Life is teaching me well! ✸

Q. *Why do we celebrate Thanksgiving? Is this strictly a "Pilgrims and Indians" celebration, or is there a deeper meaning?*

A. On the Higher Spiritual Planes, this has always been a time when the Angels and Great Beings have looked back over the past year and gathered together the "Harvest" of Man's accumulated good (his lessons learned), and placed them before the Spiritual Hierarchy. This is a great feasting time and celebration, when our guides and teachers are able to report the progress being made here on earth. *It is called The Festival of Gratitude.*

The Pilgrims were, for the most part, highly evolved souls who intuitively remembered the Cosmic Harvest celebration, and so they brought forth their own Thanksgiving Feast Day in the outer world, in gratitude for the blessings God had given them.

Thanksgiving is both an inner and an outer action. In the outer world, the harvest is gathered in, and nature prepares for a dormant resting period, in preparation for the New Beginning in the Spring. Nature rests and Man also, has more rest time with the shorter days. He has a sense of peace and gratitude for another harvest gathered. He spreads a fine feast, and celebrates by breaking bread with his friends and loved ones.

In the inner world, the Christ, Angels and Masters celebrated another harvest of rapidly evolving souls. The Angels move very close to the earth and inspire Man, by their love and radiance, to express more love and brotherhood. Hence, at the holiday season we are, indeed, filled with good will and a desire to give and share.

Q. *I enjoy the beautiful decorations and trees at Christmastime, but I'm very confused about the rightness of cutting down living trees for this purpose. Would you comment please?*

A. Every part of creation worships the King and Christ is King. When you lovingly select a living tree, taking it joyously home to make it even more beautiful with lights and ornaments, the Tree Deva is proud and happy that you chose "her creation" to focalize your celebration! All nature celebrates the rebirth of the Light on earth that we recognize at Christmas. So, my friend, select your tree with love, give thanks to Nature for this beautiful creation, and enjoy the wonder of the Holy Season, knowing the tree has reached its ultimate purpose by participating in the celebration of the Christ. ☀

Q. *Why do we use trees and wreaths in our Christmas celebration?*

A. Long before the birth of Christianity, the Romans used evergreens as symbols of eternal life during their Saturnalia feast times in mid-December.

Evergreens are symbolic of the tree of Life, and man's ability to be victorious in the face of death. They symbolize Life eternal and enduring. The wreath of green, made in a circle, symbolizes man's Infinite Nature, without beginning and without end.

At the time of the Winter Solstice, when Nature has allowed her creations to die away and rest for awhile, the evergreens symbolize victory over death. And because the days then begin to lengthen and the Light returns to the earth, we celebrate the return of the Light, The Christ, by lighting candles and sharing joyously with one another. ☀

Q.   *During the Holiday season many gifts were given to me. I am very grateful and touched by the love and kindness expressed by the givers. Yet, I feel the action of the gift is, somehow, incomplete. Is there something more involved here than the receiving of a gift?*

A.   Gifts, lovingly presented, touch us in our heart centers, and warm our souls. But, for all that is received, something must be given in order to *continue* the unending flow of loving energy that passes between the lover and the beloved, whether here in our world of form, or on the Higher Planes of Spirit. The reason you feel the action incomplete is that your soul knows the Law of the Circle, giving, receiving, and then, giving again. A gift *is a seed of love* that longs for a place of planting, in yet another field, in the form of another receiver. Pass it on, my friend. For every gift received, give another to someone else. ✺

Q.   *Do you think ministers or holy women should wear makeup or jewelry?*

A.   I do! I believe we owe it to ourselves, our friends and to God to look as good as we can! Our form houses the Spirit and is the Temple of the Living God. If dressing neatly and attractively and using tasteful makeup and jewelry makes the woman feel good about herself, I think she owes it to herself to do so. God is the Creator of Beauty. Is not Woman, also, a creator of beauty? People who are offended by makeup, attractive dress, etc., are still in the Dark Ages of religion where their version of God was forbidding and demanding. Spirituality allows the soul to celebrate the God of Love and beauty by practicing these principles themselves. ✺

Q.   *Several times lately I've dreamed about getting married, but I'm not sure who I was marrying. What do you think this means?*

A.   One of the most powerful dream symbols you can have is that of marriage. To be a bride, in your dreams, is to make union with your own higher (Christ) self. *The reason you don't see the face of your bridegroom is because you don't yet see the Christ within yourself.* But the reoccurring imagery of marriage behind the veil of sleep strongly indicates your soul is yearning for that spiritual union, and when your personality self sleeps, the contact is being made! The symbol of marriage in our dreamtime is an indicator of our place on the spiritual path. Birth, death and marriage are the important major steps of life. To dream of birth is to awaken in a new conciousness. To dream of death is symbolizing the dying away of old worn out beliefs. And to dream of marriage is the souls longing for union with God. To me, the dreams of being a bride, or watching a wedding, bring great joy and encouragement. They indicate that on a soul level, it is well with my Being, and I am moving closer and closer to experiencing union with my God-self! Dream on, beautiful seeker, for each nights experience as the bride (or bridegroom) brings you closer to the Mystical Marriage with God! ☀

Q. *I've appreciated your Q. & A. about dreams, and now I have one for you. Why do I constantly dream of being in the frozen North, or where there is a lot of ice and snow? I even wake up cold from these dreams sometimes.*

A. Ice is always the symbol of a frozen or locked condition, usually having to do with emotional patterns. To see things frozen and cold is to view one's life and circumstances in rigid or frozen form. To be surrounded by snow and ice indicates the need for the dreamer to get in touch with their true feelings, and to allow the warmth of love and kindness to enter more into their life experiences and relationships. Often unforgiven situations will freeze the emotional body, and the individual becomes cold and devoid of loving energies, resulting in anger and fear and sorrow. The dreamer in the frozen situation needs to "thaw out" emotionally and let the life-giving sun of Love bring warmth and joy into their being! ✹

Q. *I've had several dreams about being at a ballgame. I keep wanting to get into the game, but I always wake up before I get to bat. What's going on here?*

A. You are being urged to learn "how to play the game of Life", which must be played joyfully and fairly. Your frustration of never getting up to bat shows defensive and competitive traits that I'm sure you are being urged to correct.

Behind sleep at night, we are often shown our weaknesses so that we can overcome them. When your competitive nature and sense of being "overlooked" have been brought into greater harmony with the rhythm of Life, the dreams will either stop, or you'll finally get up to bat. ☀

Q. *I often dream I am sewing, or making a new dress. I might mention I can't even thread a needle in my waking state. Can you shed some light on this?*

A. My friend, it is a beautiful dream that indicates you are busy, busy, busy working behind sleep. What this means is that behind sleep at night, in your etheric body, you travel to the lower planes of darkness, and there you are busy mending the tattered garments of those souls who have lost their way in darkness and you are helping them create new garments (of Light). At the same time, every moment spent in that unselfish service is helping you create a more beautiful spiritual garment (body) as part of your own spiritual initiation! ☀

Q. *I keep having dreams about not being able to find my shoes. What do you think I'm being told to do?*

A. Anything having to do with the feet, in dream symbology, is concerned with our spiritual progress and our understanding. Therefore, shoes are symbolic of our ability to "get on the Path" and go forward. Lost or misplaced shoes mean we are "dragging our feet" and not taking advantage of all of our opportunities to advance. The fact that we search for the shoes indicates the soul's desire to "get on with it".

The fact that this comes as a repetitive dream would signify obstacles on the subconscious level that prevent the dreamer from rapid advancement. The subconscious will continue to symbolically show the blockage until the dreamer awakens into more understanding. Summing up, I would say you want to " get on the road" but ego won't allow you at this time to recognize a weakness in your belief system; therefore if you can't find your shoes, you can't go!

Look deep within your own Inner Self, and ask to be shown the portion that is out of alignment with your perfect Divine Plan. Meditate upon true understanding of the situation just before retiring. It is very likely the dream will return with greater clarifiction. ✸

Q. *I have some awful dreams of being chased. They never catch me in the dreams, but I'm very frightened. Can you shed light on this?*

A. When we dream of being pursued by some shadowy "unknown" figure, it usually indicates deep feelings of having wronged another, and the need to be caught and punished. Our submerged feelings of guilt will pursue us, one way or another, until we've forgiven ourselves and rid ourselves of the old "sin and guilt" trip. Your pursuer is your own hidden guilt. Whether from this or a past lifetime, the chase goes on until you forgive and release it all into the Light! ✺

Q. *Please remark about rubies. I've really been drawn to them. I dreamed I was given a handful of raw rubies, and in another dream I was wearing a beautiful ruby pendant. Is someone trying to tell me something?*

A. Color, such as ruby red, contains the highest vibrational sensitivity in the light or vision spectrum. Ruby red color is healing, energizing, peacegiving and healthgiving. Color penetrates consciousness inoffensively, and lifts, soothes, and exalts. The more spiritually sensitive you are, the more you are the recipient of spiritual emanations from colors.

The Ruby contains the vibrations of Christ Love and power. One perfect ruby condensed into a jewel contains the power of spirit far beyond our mortal creations. The ruby is constantly changing our consciousness of Life and of God's perfection!

When you begin to dream about rubies you are undergoing night time initiations into the Way of the Heart, to teach you to become more sensitive and caring about others. It is, in many legends and myths, the badge of honor and right action. To wear a ruby signifies that you are becoming an Initiate of the Life Force and the traveler upon the pathway of honor, integrity, beauty, gentleness and Universal Love. Henceforth, Life will offer you many opportunities to learn these lessons. The spiritual traveler must earn, by day to day actions, the right to wear the ruby.

Just as the red rose awakens the Divine senses to Universal selflessness and beauty, the ruby stone stimulates the physical senses to integrate these same qualities. As you know, "As above, so below" is our desire, and ultimate fulfillment here in the great University of Life called Planet Earth! ☀

Q. *I know you must get tired of always being asked about dreams, but I've had one that has been puzzling me for a long time. I frequently dream of policemen! Does this mean I'm destined for legal troubles in the future?*

A. No, no, no! A policeman in a dream is a Guardian Angel, representing the Cosmic Laws of Right Action!

To be chased by a policeman (angel) is a strong reminder that the dreamer is breaking the Laws of God. If corrective action isn't taken immediately, a karmic retribution will confront the dreamer in some form in their physical life in the very near future.

To be watched by a policeman (angel) is a reminder that you aren't alone, and God really does know that you are here! It is reassurance of Divine Protection.

If the policeman (angel) looks angry or threatening, you are being reminded that your relationship with your guardian is in trouble because of your own actions.

If the policeman (angel) stops you and gives you a ticket, your karma is about to descend, and cannot be avoided. (Much prayer to the intercessory angels would definitely be recommended)!

If a policeman (angel) helps you across the street, or over an obstacle you are, again, being assured of much divine protection in your physical life!

If you talk to the policeman (angel) you are being assured you have a very good relationship with your guardian angel.

Just remember, policeman in the dream worlds are always our protective guardian angels. They represent the Divine Will of the Laws of God.

Q. *I dreamed I was a bear and I was all alone. I couldn't find anyone else like myself. This has really troubled me. I wondered if you had any insights into the meaning of this dream.*

A. The bear hibernates, and hides away during the winter (stormy) season. Are you being told that you fail to communicate or share with others in your times of stress and strife? Hibernators don't make much effort to have warm relationships, and often hide away within themselves. They fear intimate situations, and hide their tender side. They often growl, criticizing others rather than being loving and supportive. They find fault, and "act like an old bear" when someone tries to get close. Are you the loner, not allowing close companionships? Are you the bear that grumbles and growls when brought into intimate situations? Could the dream be a warning of your need to be more loving, and companionable? ✿

Q.   *In dreams, I often find myself wandering in and out of houses. Some are familiar, but most are not.   Exactly what does a house mean? And is the color important? I have dreamed of being in a bright red house several times recently.*

A.   Houses represent how we are living our lives at this time. The basement usually stands for the sub-conscious, or hidden part of our selves. Here the past errors (karma) are hidden and the dreamer is being reminded to "know thyself". The main floor relates to our conscious every day world, or the outer portion of our lives. The second floor relates to our personality and ego selves, or how we think of ourselves. Here one meets symbols of ego, willfulness and pride, two stumbling blocks that we must overcome in order to evolve. The highest floor or attic is of higher consciousness and represents the parts of ourselves we've not yet uncovered.

In dreams, when we keep returning to a familiar house over and over, it indicates that we are investigating our own feelings and desires. It is a constant "prodding" to rectify, heal and balance the emotions.

The color of the house means a great deal. It represents our strong judgments and feelings which are "coloring" our consciousness. For instance, a red house represents anger, and often denotes danger or karma that is about to erupt in our life. Each color symbolizes a specific condition or virtue that needs to be addressed in our earthly learning process.

To dream of a beautiful house signifies the beauty of our soul's journey, and our Higher aspirations. A hovel, on the other hand, represents our "spiritual bankrupcy" and a need to "clean up our act". ✸

Q. *Why do I dream of the world being torn apart by earth-quakes? Is that prophetic? Does it indicate a terrible earth-quake coming somewhere?*

A. It *could* be prophetic for you, but it is highly unlikely that it is for the *earth*. Earthquakes in dreams usually denote your world (your understanding) is about to be abruptly changed. It can indicate karma descending unexpectedly. It is usually a warning that your personal world is going to undergo change, and that your old belief systems are about to be disrupted. It often means a tragedy or sorrow will touch your life in the immediate future, something that will descend upon you unexpectidly. Pay attention. ☀

Q. *I dreamed my family Bible fell apart in my hands. The pages were yellow and torn as if very old. What does this mean?*

A. The image of religious writings, yellowed with age and falling apart, speaks of old worn-out concepts of belief that need to be updated or renewed. Old belief systems that speak of judgment, sin, fear, death and hell need to be replaced with a higher understanding of forgiveness, love and immortality. Look not so much to what was written in the ancient past, but see the Christ within each living moment now! A Bible falling apart particularly states the need for renewal, for the old no longer sustains you. ☀

Q. *I constantly see, in dreams and in meditations, beautiful hues of rose and pink. What special significance do these colors have?*

A. When the Door of the Heart opens and the soul begins to feel and experience true tenderness and love, it is said we begin to "look through rose colored glasses". In other words, the rosy hues of love colors our waking states and dreamtimes! To see these colors frequently indicates your inner guides and Teachers are showing you the more loving side of yourself, and of Life in general.

There is a great significance in seeing color in a dream or meditative experience. The colors each carry certain God qualities and powers. To see specific colors in repetitive patterns means you are learning lessons and developing an understanding of these powers. Rose shows the soul is learning compassion, mercy, sympathy, empathy, and affection. Soft pink indicates the souls yearning for reverence, devotion and love. ✹

Q. *I keep dreaming of being in the midst of wars and battles. It's never the same battle, but I just keep dreaming of being engaged in combat. What do you think it means?*

A. I believe it represents a battle or struggle with your ego and will. The one who has controlled others in past lifetimes by will power must eventually learn not to do this. It is often taught behind sleep, in the dream state. To be in a battle with many enemies indicates that one is in the midst of resolving past Karma relating to the attempted enslavement of many in past lifetimes. Surrender to Divine Will, and forgiving of oneself and others, will often bring the nocturnal battles to an end. When the lesson has been learned and the soul no longer seeks to control or impose its will on others the wars can end. ✺

Q. *I dream of using guns, and sometimes of making a gun. I am not a "gun freak" so why do I have these dreams?*

A. Dreams and thoughts of weapons such as guns means the soul is seeking to overcome violent tendencies. Guns often represent vicious, cruel words, and angry retorts. These words can kill just the same as a physical weapon, for they kill dreams, hopes and self esteem. There are many ways to express violence in one's nature. Repeated dreams of weapons indicates the soul, with the help of the Inner Guide, is trying to overcome the need to lash out and hurt others. ✺

Q. *I've become aware of so many beautiful things recently. Particularly, I'm seeing rainbows everywhere. Does that mean anything spiritual or special?*

A. The rainbow is God's promise of His ongoing love and protection. To see rainbows is to be reminded that we are very beloved children of God, and protégés of angels and saints. Each of the colors project healing energies, and to be "bathed" in rainbow consciousness, is to receive night time healing from the angels. This means that your awareness of the Creator's symbology permits you to "see" or "tune into" their essence more readily.

The Blue of the rainbow denotes faith, power, and spirituality. Yellow is the wisdom. Red is vitality and strength. Green is balance and healing. Orange is wisdom and health. The violet color is transformation and freedom. Breathe in the essence of each color, and experience it inwardly. Fill your world with rainbows and crystals, for they are God's eternal promise of love and foreverness! Yes, something spiritual is happening! You are being reborn into your spiritual nature.

Q. *You have always been able to give me such wonderful insights into my dreams. Where did you learn so much about dreams and their meanings?*

A.   I was a devotee of the late Ann Ree Colton for many years, and her teachings taught me *how* to look into the inner meaning of dreams and vision. I've used her marvelous book *"Watch your Dreams"* as a guide-line and inspiration for over twenty years. I highly recommend it to all who are truly serious about understanding the soul's "language of the night"!

It was in my own deep meditations that I was finally taught the "Code" of nighttime messages, and from there on, it was fairly simple. To this day I wonder if I would have been so successful in my interpertations without her wonderful teachings. One thing is for certain, Ann Ree Colton was a teacher I'll never forget!

Q. *Exactly what is a tithe?*

A. A tithe is spiritual seeding of our garden of prosperous and joyous living! It is a gift of gratitude for Life and our on going blessings. Started under Abraham, a giving of the first portion of the harvest to the temple activated the Cosmic Law of Ten fold return. It was a physical demonstration that God was the Supplier, and we, in giving back a portion, acknowledged from whence cometh our good.

There are two kinds of tithe, a temple tithe and a community tithe. The temple tithe is the freely given portion of our supply to the place where we receive our spiritual inspiration. It is a gift of gratitude and must be given joyously, freely, clearly unencumbered, in order that the spiritual works may continue. *It is not your duty, it is your privilege.* And as every farmer knows, when good seed is planted, a rich harvest is usually the result.

A community tithe is the charity we give to family, friends, neighbors and the place where we live. This is from our emotional need to be involved with making our little part of the universe better. It can be our time, talents, monies, materials, etc. The resultant good feeling of contributing to the helping of the community rewards us in many different ways. As we learn to give and share we, in turn feel better about ourselves, and experience peace, joy and self satisfaction.

Both tithes are essential; the temple tithe is the true activation of God's laws to "give unto Me thy first portion and I will return unto you blessing heaped up and running over"!

Beware that you don't give your tithe as a bribe, for the Universe cannot be bribed, manipulated or bought. Acknowledge God (All-Good) as the only source of our abundance and in gratitude give the first portion. In the doing, we activate the Cosmic storehouse of blessings. ☀

Q. *Why is it necessary to tithe?*

A. We are like cups. Unless we pour out a part therein, the cup gets full and can receive no more, and we stop receiving. A garden cannot grow unless seeds are planted. If you would reap a harvest of abundance, fullness and prosperity, you must, like a gardener, plant your seeds. A pump, when left for long periods of idleness, loses its prime. If we fail to give back to Life a portion of our substance, our "pump" may easily lose its "prime". Then we begin to feel impoverished and lacking.

God is our Source, and as we give into His loving service our tithe, or tenth of what we have received, we plant seeds to reap ever greater harvest of His Good.

The tithe symbolizes man's acknowledgment of God as his Source. As we return the tenth to the Source by giving to those who inspire us spiritually, the seeds of many fold return are planted. When seeds are planted, harvest results. If you are receiving no harvest, take a look. Have you planted your good seeds in your garden of life?

Q. *What affirmation or prayer would be good to use with my tithe or giving?*

A. You could say "I richly give and I richly receive"! or "Thank you, Father, for permitting me to be Thy instrument of giving"! Or to counter-act any fear of loss: "Thank you Father, for Thy abundance and prosperity that blesses me in return"! And as you say these words, feel and know that it is so!

Q. *I promised to tithe to my church, and I never did. Now I feel guilty because I've let the church down. Would you comment, please?*

A. Our word or promise is a sacred bond, and should never be given lightly. As for instance your promise to tithe. Tithing is a gift of love to the Universe. It is a great privilege, and an act of placing complete and total trust in the Creator. All good shall come unto you as it has been "seeded" by you! To make a promise to tithe to an organization, and then fail to keep that pledge, is not a betrayal to that organization. It is a betrayal to the Indwelling God.

There is no giving that is not a service to the Creator. When we give our sacred vow, and promise to do something, it isn't a singular action. It is a triune action between you, and the one you promise, and the God of your Being! Your word, duly witnessed and sealed by your Indwelling Presence, is how you plant the seeds for all of your future harvest. If your seeds (words) aren't good and true, how do you expect to reap a rich harvest of good?

Think about the vows you make. Is it time to save money, give money, lose weight, stop smoking or, perhaps to be more considerate and loving? Do you speak these words just to hear the sound of your own voice? Or to impress other people? Or do you vow and affirm an action, determined to follow through? *Your word is your bond*, and the Light made manifest through you. If your bond has no validity, and no one else's does, either, then what kind of a world can we possibly create for our tomorrows?

For promises broken or forgotten, forgive yourself. That is over now, it's past. And, from this moment on, be more fully aware of how very sacred is your word, and let your future pledges be a special bond between you and your God Presence! ☀

Q. *I know there must be a way to live abundantly and joyously, but I can't seem to get the formula right. Any suggestions?*

A. It is the Father's good will to give you the Kingdom, and abundance, peace, love and joy can be yours everyday. A few simple rules that might guide your consciousness toward accepting that truth are as follows:

1. *First, there must be a **desire** to change.*
2. *You must believe that you **can** change.*
3. *Start **visualizing** what you hope to accomplish. Begin to see yourself prosperous and joyous, instead of sad and bankrupt.*
4. *Acknowledge that you are **deserving** of good, that you are the heir of the King, not the bond servant.*
5. *Begin **expecting** miracles, and expecting good, to happen to you.*
6. ***Make your tithe**, for these are the seeds for great harvest. Give spontaneously and expansively with a sense of joy!*
7. *Give the **best** you have to offer into work, relationships, life, and fill your consciousness with Hope.*
8. ***Be kind** to yourself. **Love yourself**, as you would have the Universe love and nurture you.*
9. ***Stop criticizing others**; work, instead on yourself and your attitudes.*
10. ***Take the first step. Do something good for someone else**, unconditionally, and without any expectations, just do it for the sheer joy of doing it!*

These are simple steps, but they are moving in the right direction to make changes in your life. We are each responsible for our own little part of the universe, and it's up to us to create either our own chaos or cosmos. When we are ignorant of our creative abilities, and think and feel negatively, then destructive, unhappy actions follow. When we *embrace Truth*, and begin to *discipline our thoughts*, tempering them with tolerance, compassion and love, then order emerges.

We aren't victims of a capricious "Fate", being struck down for no apparent reason. We are, instead, learning how to be "Gods" and how to create a heaven here on earth. As we make choices, we build our world, thought by thought.

I've recommended these books several times, but again would remind you of the valued wisdom's of:

The Game of Life by Florence Scovill Shinn.

The Power of your Spoken Word by Florence Scovill Shinn.

The Prosperity Secret of the Ages by Catherine Ponder.

The Mystical "I" by Joel Goldsmith.

The Celestine Prophecy by James Redfield

Q.   *I am really confused about my spiritual attitudes toward money and possessions. If I experience abundance, I feel guilt because so many people are in need. If I'm broke I feel guilty because somehow I'm not living according to God's Laws of Good. Consequently, money is my most confusing issue. Would you comment, please?*

A.   Anxiety seizes you whether you have money or you don't have money. Wouldn't it seem that *anxiety*, more than money, is the issue? You worry when you have it and when you don't have it, so it appears anxiety (stress) is deeply rooted in your belief system. In reality, money has very little to do with how you are feeling and reacting. It is all right to feel concern when you don't have money. But when you worry, either way it shows that a deep inner feeling of anxiety has a strong hold in your subconscious mind.

You have no need to feel guilty about money. Money is only an energy that is meant to facilitate your life in this world. When you are eating, do you feel guilty about the food? When you bathe or drink, are you guilty about the water? When you sleep, are you guilty about your bed? Then why would you feel guilty if you have money to pay your bills or buy your food or take a vacation? The question of guilt does not arise with food, water, clothes, and beds, for they are necessities. What then is money? Is it not a necessity for passage through our normal life experiences? You have no reason to ever be guilty about money. Remain even minded when you have much *and* when you have little.

Change your attitudes about money and possessions. Keep with you all that you need for everyday living. God is not resentful if you have much, nor is God miserly. It is the Father's very good pleasure that you have all that you are *capable of receiving!*

Neither should you feel guilty about another's lack. It is every soul's opportunity to learn about the truth of manifestation, and you cannot learn for another. You can only learn for yourself.

Bless your good, for it will, by the Law of Attraction, create more good! Continue to feel anxiety and guilt, and like a curse, you will drive your abundance away from you! ☀

Q.   *How do I learn attitudes of abundance?*

A.   The Divine Principle, call it your Angel, if you wish, honors and prospers the one who has learned to love life, who works and serves joyously, gives freely, experiences gratitude for even the little things and is nonjudgmental, and not jealous and resentful of others good fortune. The one honored by the Angel of Abundance has no fear or anger toward others, nor asks "Whats in it for me"? The honored one opens to the peace, beauty, harmony and love of God, and as He freely gives, the Law of Attraction draws back to him great blessings.

To learn attitudes of abundance, look at every day as a *great opportunity to grow and learn.* Work! Do something for someone else! Give! Share! The joy that will flood your being will create a magnetic attraction to draw back to you wondrous good.

The Angel of Abundance *never* dwells in the energy field of the lazy, self-pitying, angry, fearful, jealous, or ungrateful!

Change these attitudes to love, beauty, harmony, peace, forgiveness and willingness to serve, and the Angel of Abundance will dwell with you forever. ☼

Q. *I'm terrified of death. What is wrong with me?*

A. Your fear of death shows that you identify yourself as *body,* and *not as spirit.* You are eternal spirit that has always been and always shall be. Death is life's greatest experience, as we move out of one dimension into another, to express our eternalness on yet another plane. What is wrong is that you worship the false god of Personality (body) and know not of the true God (Spirit). You accept shadows and illusions (body) and are blinded to true substance (the God Presence) that is your reality.

"Death, where is thy sting"? There is none, for, in Truth, death is not a condition of the great Reality of Spirit, it is only a condition created out of our ignorance, fear and dispair. When we know God as the All-In-All, and ourselves as part of the same, death is no longer a threatening force from the shadows, but a passageway to a higher, brighter plane. Center your thoughts on Life, my friend, the loving Creator has no "horrible surprises" waiting to terrify you. Only more love, more life, more joy! For that is the nature of God! ✺

Q. *What kind of lessons can a soul learn from a terrifying illness like cancer?*

A.   When an individual has been given a terminal diagnosis, then the real learning begins. The soul that is truly surrendered to God, really believing that there is no death, gets the opportunity to "live" their belief system to its completion.

Often spiritual seekers believe these truths in their minds, but when they are faced with the actuality, that belief falls apart. They rant and rage against "what God has done to me", completely forgetting every experience is arranged by ourselves.

We see the difference between mortal man and divine man when the individual is brought face to face with impending death of the physical body. Mortal man becomes angry and fearful, and rages out against his fate. Divine man say, "Let me live this full experience and learn all that I can from it. Let me live in Thy peace, O God, and when my time come to drop this worn-out garment of flesh, let me return to my true home. Death cannot frighten me, for I am not of earth, I am of the Spirit. My soul is immortal, and I can never die".

The lesson is to know, even as the body is dying, that the soul can never die, for we are spirit, and we are forever. To face death peacefully, and without fear, is to cross the final frontier of life upon earth as a Master. To this end each one of us must eventually come. As long as we scream and resent death, we will continue to be born and die, again and again, until at last we finally "get it", we are immortals in God; we are everlasting spirit! Only then does death come as gently as an angel's kiss, to escort us back to our true home. Then our sojourns in this great university called Earth are completed, and we will receive our Master's degree!

Q. *Would you explain why you feel cremation is preferable to earth burial?*

A. Fire is purification, particularly of earthy matter. We are spirit, *temporarily* inhabiting flesh and blood vehicles called bodies. When the spirit (soul) departs, the earthly remains must be dealt with. Like an abandoned house or car, it no longer has value or use.

Many bodies have deteriorated through disease and abuse. It is time that we stop the barbaric practice of burying diseased, worn out bodies in our beautiful earth. The residue of disease, grief, horror and pain lingers for years around burial places, contaminating the land and the atmosphere with these negative vibrations.

Cremation is symbolic of our belief that we truly are spirit, and that leaving the worn out body is an awesome freedom! The fire purifies any residual disease so that the earth isn't contaminated. The cremation of the remains prevents thought forms of grief and sorrow being "planted" in a permanent place, a constant reminder of the loss of a loved one. Cemeteries do little to heal the earth. They remain morbid places of grief and pain, constant reminders of death. The cold stones used to honor the departed remain a constant homage to death, not to Life!

A large portion of the world today believes in cremation. As we become more enlightened about our true spiritual nature, we will care less and less what happens to the out-grown, discarded vehicles (bodies) that we've left behind. *God fearing* people cling to the earthly remains, as if they too, must be preserved. For what? *God loving* people celebrate themselves as spirit, and left over bodies mean nothing! Tossing the ashes to the winds symbolizes our belief that they are still alive and free, just in another realm. And it is a loving act of setting them free from all earthly bindings! ☀

Q. *How long should one wait before cremating the body?*

A. We recommend that the body be left undisturbed for 72 hours (three days). The Masters tell us it takes that long for the Gathering Angels to retrieve all the soul records from the body. The light of soul in the eyes, the divine spark in the heart, the karmic records in the blood, and the soul patterns stored in the cells all must be gathered and returned to the spiritual planes. After that, cremation may take place at any time.

Sometimes the seventy two hour wait isn't possible, as when a body is destroyed in a violent action, or has a contagious disease. There are other means of gathering the records under those circumstances, but is a much more complicated process. It often causes the one who has passed on anxious moments, for fear that all of their necessary records can't be retrieved. The 72 hour wait simply allows us to work in greater co-operation with the angels and our departed ones. ❁

Q. *If I cremate my loved one, then where can I go in my grief to feel close to them?*

A. By going within, quietly and prayerfully, you can certainly "feel close", for memories are wonderful things. But, if you need an actual place, why don't you put a bench in your garden where you can pray, meditate and remember? Or plant a tree or a flower in their memory? Perhaps you can make a donation of a tree or a shrub to a local park or garden? A donation to a special charity warms the heart of the remembering one. ❁

Q. *So many funeral notices say send no flowers. Is that a good or bad thing to do?*

A. Flowers used in the death ritual enable the angels to work as comforters and sustainers for those who grieve. To omit flowers for the dead produces an empty, cold ritual. The fragrance and beauty of flowers during a ritual of death brings much comfort and healing to those who mourn. The angels use the flower essences to try to heal the aura of sorrow and grief. When the mourners behold the beauty and smell the sweet floral fragrance, they are accepting a comforting blessing from the angels, and from God.

At funerals, the fragrances, colors and love with which they were given bring remembrance of Life Everlasting, and not just an ending.

For ages, flowers have been used in rituals and celebrations by those who are caring and knowing. This is because intuitively they are aware that flowers are close to the soul within all living things. ✸

Q. *I am aware of your love of roses. What do they represent to you? And what is your favorite color of rose?*

A. Roses to me, other than humans, are God's most glorious creation. Their perfection is symbolic of the true beauty of the divine man, locked away in human form (the tightly closed bud). Warmed by the sun (father) and nurtured by the earth (mother), they blossom forth in beauty beyond mortal man's ability to create. No mortal artist can paint such perfection!

I think roses are a gift of Grace, and it is said that where roses are evil cannot exist. Looking at a rose garden I can believe it is truly so.

My favorite roses? Pink roses touch my heart so tenderly. Yellow roses make me smile with joy. ✹

Q   *How does the soul depart the body at death?*

A.   I have been shown three ways that this happens. For those who still "sleep", without knowledge of their responsibility for the raising of the race to a higher consciousness, the soul will depart from the *solar plexus* and will return into a place without great soul light, or to what we call the lower astral plane. It is there that they will continue their experiences until it is time to come back and try to raise the consciousness again, through another life experience.

The *Truth* students who are endeavoring to find a reason for living, and who accept a responsibility for their brothers and sisters, begin to raise their energy to the *heart*, and will go to what we call the higher astral plane where there is much light, and much greater opportunity for the soul to continue it's progression and growth.

But for the spiritual seeker who is endeavoring in every portion of life to attain a consciousness of Christ, their energy is at a much higher level. At the moment of death, when these souls leave the body they will leave through the *head*, and go quickly to the plane of sublime light where the Christ is, uniting with the Masters and the angels, and where great work can be done, not only for the departing one, but for those left behind.

Q. *I've appreciated so much all that you have shared about life after death, grief, etc. I know you are asked many times to do rites of passage when someone dies, but I'm not sure I know what that means. Would you share an example or two of some kind of rites that someone like me could do, please?*

A.   Each one of us, at sometime or another, will experience the death of a loved one. There is no other time in our lives that we will feel so helpless. We want to do something, but numbed by grief and fear, most of us feel "frozen", and ineffective.

I can share with you three different ceremonies that anyone can do following the passing of a loved one. These are services that can be done in private or in a gathering of many. Not only do these rituals bring comfort to the living, they render great assistance to the departing soul. These are simply suggestions and each one usually will add their own touches, as Spirit directs them. Feel free to improvise! ✸

A Single Candle Ritual for 7 Days

(1)   Light a 15 hour candle, placing it on a side table or the mantle. (I recommend placing a small bowl or saucer under it to catch drippings, and a glass chimney over it).

(2)   Place a snapshot or picture of your loved one next to it.

(3)   Write a prayer on a simple white card and place it on the other side of the candle example:

"Beloved Father-God, into your blessed peace and Light I commend _____ (name). Enfold him/her in love and guide him/her safely home to your perfect Heaven. I know _____(name) is a beloved child of God, and I rejoice in his/her homecoming"
Amen
Each time you pass the candle, repeat the prayer silently or aloud.

(4)   Do this for seven consecutive days to help your beloved one make their journey home.

(5)   Each time the prayer is done, the departing one will feel a great warmth of love and encouragement, which greatly aids them on their Homeward journey.

Eight Candle Ceremony

The items you will need for this ceremony are:

❶ A simple table or altar covered with a white, blue or pink cloth. Use natural materials, such as silk, cotton, linen or a mostly natural fiber blend.

❷ 7 small white candles and 1 taller white candle.

❸ A picture of the deceased.

❹ Flowers.

❺ A Bible or whatever else holds special meaning for you.

❻ Soft, sacred music playing in the background.

With these items you are ready to begin.

(1)   Line the candles up with the largest one on the right end of the line up. Light all of the small candles leaving the largest one unlit.

(2)   As you face the altar, pray, then read a sacred or spiritual passage. At this time you or someone else might give a short eulogy and state the purpose of the gathering, which is to help release the departing soul from the bonds of earth. As you speak the following words before each candle, extinguish the flame.

1st Candle: Dearest _____(name), we now see all bindings released from your feet. In the name of the Christ (God) you are set free from the physical bounds of earth. You are free!

(extinguish the first candle)

2nd Candle: We release you now from all earthly responsibilities to myself, family and friends. You are free!

(extinguish the second candle)

3rd Candle: We release you now from all longings for earthly things.

You are free!

(extinguish third candle)

4th Candle: We release you from all emotions of this earthly plane. You are free!

(extinguish fourth candle)

5th Candle: We release you from all thoughts that bind you to earthly things. You are free!

(extinguish fifth candle)

6th Candle: We release you from all unfinished business of the earth. All is forgiven. All is well. You are free!

(extinguish sixth candle)

7th Candle: We release you from all visions of earthly things. This day may you open new eyes to a new spiritually transformed *you*. Behold the glories of Heaven, beloved_____! You are free!

(extinguish seventh candle)

Light the Eighth Candle

Now, beloved _____, may your grand new life begin in heaven. This candle represents the great Christ Light that you are. You are free! You are free! You are free.

Amen

A 21 Day Prayer Vigil

You will need a long burning white candle, a picture of the deceased and an intention to do this ritual for 21 days.

(1) Place the lit candle in a safe place, preferable with a glass chimney around it, away from children and heavy traffic.

(2) Place the photo of the deceased near the candle.

(3) Keep the candle burning around the clock for a full twenty one days. As one candle diminishes, light another from the flame. (If it goes out, simply light it again.)

(4) Daily sit before the candle, praying for your loved one. In your quiet time encourage the departed soul to

"Keep moving into the white light! You can do it! You are Light! You are Love! Don't turn back, keep moving onward and upward into the Pure Bright Light of God! Don't worry about me (us); we're going to be all right. Go into the White Light. That is where you belong now. Everything is all right"!

Like an earthly cheering section, mentally and verbally, keep encouraging the departed one to travel onward into the Light of God. In prayer, ask the Angels, guides, teachers, and Christ to welcome your loved one Home!

Each time you do this, they get a "cosmic boost" and your love helps them make a tranquil and loving journey. They can hear you. Love travels *instantly* between the worlds.

Send Light! Send Love!
Send Prayers!

Q. *Where do you get your wisdoms?*

A.   I seek to live as completely in the Light as possible, and when I need information, I go directly to that Light, God, rather than to someone who merely reflects their own personal understanding of Light. The Nature of God is Love, Truth and Power, available to every single soul upon this planet, if they are willing to go within and be still enough to listen, Light from the true Source, God, is a wisdom that cannot be denied, nor can it be purchased, stolen or forced. Only by surrender and stillness can the voice of Wisdom be heard. That wisdom is so clear, and in-depth, that not only is it easily understandable, but also simple to teach and share with others. Wisdom, powered by God's Love, leaves no room for confusion or intellectual babbling. I seek the Divine Mind that is God, and know the Creator is my source. ✸

Q.   *You so often refer to the "I Am" teachings. Please explain what you mean by this.*

A.   Contemplating "I Am" as anything and everything you wish to be, it is one of the mightiest means of releasing the Inner God Power, Love, Wisdom and Truth that man is capable of using!

"I Am" is the starter button within the heart of every individualized entity on earth. When you qualify that divine, creative energy by your personal instruction, you put in motion an infallible law. Therefore, when you say "I am tired, broke, or lonely", immediately a sense of being exactly that fills your being, and at that moment, you have created and accepted loneliness, tiredness and poverty.

In the "I Am" teachings we become aware of the divine power within that is constantly creating our daily moment-by-moment reality. From such awareness comes an intense desire to qualify that great "I Am" energy in a much more positive way. Therefore, "I Am Joyous"! "I Am Prosperous"! "I Am filled with energy and feel great"! replaces our old creations of dispair, anguish, fear and impoverishment.

Too much emphasis cannot be placed upon the importance of contemplating, as often as possible, the "I Am" as the Mighty Active Presence of God within you, your home, your world, and all of your affairs. Every thought, indeed every breath, is God in Action in You! You have free will, and it is entirely up to you, to *qualify* your thoughts and feelings, either positively or negatively, and to determine how your personal little world shall act for you!

"I Am the Resurrection and the Life"! What a powerful statement! The "I Am" in you can be qualified with so much love and positive energy that you, literally, can be resurrected from a living death to a , joyous immortality! Try it! You might like it!

You might consider, on a daily basis, using some of the following "I Am" statements, and watch your attitudes and relationships change, for you will be creating your "heaven right here on earth". Repetition creates Power!

"I Am the resurrection and the Life"!

"I Am joyously meeting life and all of my opportunities to grow and learn"!

"I Am perfect health. Every cell, fiber, organ, muscle and tissue of my body is filled with perfection"!

"I Am loved! I Am loving. I Am love"!

"I Am manifesting abundance and good supply. All of my earthly needs are promptly filled by the Mighty I Am Power of God"!

"I Am God's intelligence and Wisdom manifesting in all of my decisions and actions"!

"I Am the obedient, intelligent activity in this mind and body"!

"I Am Divine Justice and order in all of my affairs"!

"I Am the energy used in every action"!

"I Am God's strength and power, and the ability to apply it in all of my affairs"!

"I Am the completeness of all perfection you ever want to manifest"!

"I Am Love, the Mighty Motivator of every action"!

"I Am the Truth that sets you free"!

And so it is.

* " I Am" is an etymology of the name for God first given (Exodus 4:14) to Moses: JHVH (Pronounced "Yahweh") *"I Am that I Am"* (This name appears throughout the Old Testament, but in our English translations it has been substituted with the word Lord). The words "I Am" create a multileveled bridge of conciousness uniting the seemingly separated individualized " I am" of each self with the power, wisdom, love and oneness of the Divine "I Am", and use of these words enable us to unlock this energy, as Jesus did, and direct it forth in great blessing to do the works of God on earth. ☀

Q. *In February 1985 I was privileged to hear you give a stirring message called I Am there. Is that message available at this time?*

A. As you no doubt remember, it was used in the closing of a worship service. I am happy to share it again.

I Am There

Hear my words, O child of my Inmost Heart! Your way is duly noted, and much aid do I send to you as you journey in consciousness ever onward. Your destiny did I set before you began this earthly odyssey, and I have not sent you forth alone.

When the shadows seem dark and fearful around you, and you do not hear my voice,
I Am There.
When you join the cosmic dance and your heart soars in joyous freedom,
I Am There.
When you tarry, and seem to lose your way,
I Am There.
For you are Heart of My Heart, and Light of My Light. You are the beloved of My Being! I will forever guide and show you the Way, if you but seek Me. In your heart I dwell, as you dwell in Mine!
And I Am Always There!
Truly, before your sojourn began, it was meant that you would find the temple door, and thrice would ask to enter in. Long have you searched, and now is the door ready to open, that I might welcome you into the Inner Sanctum where you will find My rest and comfort! At last the time has come! Seek and you will find! Knock and the door will open,
For I Am There!
Now I will tear away your illusions and tattered garments of fear and dis-

*belief! I will clothe you in My Peace and Beauty, and bestow wondrous
blessings upon you. Beyond your mortal dreams, My Vision now opens
unto you, and as you grow, you are empowered by My Spirit! My angels
roll away the hurting obstacles and My comforter comes to bring you
unto Me,*

For I Am There!

*Be not concerned with doing, but rejoice in being. In the silence, indeed
you hear Me. And in the hustle of your market place,
you will see Me; in the thunder of the dawn you find Me;
in the noonday and in the night seek Me,*

For I Am There.

*I Am the music without beginning, I am the song and I am the singer. I
Am the dream and I Am the dreamer. I Am the gentle
caressing breeze and the thunder of your storms! I Am the night, and I
Am the stars that light your way.
I Am the Light forever and
evermore!*

For I Am There.

*I Am the Truth that sets you free. I Am the love that gives you Life! I Am
thee, and thou art Me, and we are One! Thou art beloved of my heart,
and my "forever" child. My angels walk beside you.
When you tarry and seem not to move, they stand and wait.
When you race with Life, they run beside you!
Thou art My Beloved.
Thou art My Miracle!
Thou art forever!
And so it is*

For I Am There!

About the Author

Marian Young Starnes lives in the Blue Ridge Mountains of North Carolina. She is co-founder of Terra Nova Center, a non-denominational retreat center, and is a well known lecturer and spiritual counselor. She is the publisher of *Crystals of Light,* a quarterly newsletter, which covers many different aspects of individual spiritual development.

Her down-to-earth approach to ordinary day-to-day problems has endeared her to thousands. When asked to describe her ministry, she shrugs and says " I guess I teach practical spirituality". Born intuitive and clairvoyant, she down plays her psychic gifts, and considers herself a minister and a seeker.

Marian has written hundreds of articles about the practical, day-to-day Life experiences that the sincere spiritual seeker encounters on their Homeward journey. She is a strong believer in the divine part of Humankind, and her favorite, and most frequently used maxim is *"If you can dream it, you can do it"*! This is her first book.

The Beginning......

ORDER FORM

To order additional copies of

Letters from Summerland

A Bridge Between The Worlds

Please complete the form below and send along with check or money order to:

Terra Nova
PUBLISHING

P.O. Box 669 • Cedar Mountain, NC 28718

Name:_____

Address:_____

City_____**St:**_____**Zip**_____

Phone:_____

How many books are you ordering?_____

Amount Enclosed:_____

- **1-5 Books** $16.95 each
- **6 or more**   15% discount
- **Shipping and Handling** $3.00

- **Canadian** $23.00
- **Shipping & Handling** $4.00

In North Carolina add 5% sales tax. Thank-You

Special Discount Rates for Wholesalers & Bookstores
For more information please contact
Terra Nova Publishing
P.O. Box 669 Cedar Mountain, NC 28718

NOTES